Sweet Revenge

Kay Rogal

CRIMSON
ROMANCE
Avon, Massachusetts

This edition published by
Crimson Romance
an imprint of F+W Media, Inc.
10151 Carver Road, Suite 200
Blue Ash, Ohio 45242

www.crimsonromance.com

Copyright © 2012 by Brenda Longstreth

ISBN 10: 1-4405-5167-7
ISBN 13: 978-1-4405-5167-3
eISBN 10: 1-4405-5147-2
eISBN 13: 978-1-4405-5147-5

This is a work of fiction.

Names, characters, corporations, institutions, organizations, events, or locales in this novel are either the product of the author's imagination or, if real, used fictitiously. The resemblance of any character to actual persons (living or dead) is entirely coincidental.

Dedication

FOR MY SONS, SETH & CHRIS, AND MY FRIENDS (YOU KNOW WHO YOU ARE)
WHO HAVE BEEN MY GREATEST WRITING CHEERLEADERS. . .

TO MY GRANDMOTHER, OTTOLINE, WHO PUSHED ME TO REACH
FOR THIS DREAM. . .

FOR JENNIFER, OUR CRIMSON ROMANCE EDITOR, WHO TOOK A CHANCE ON
SWEET REVENGE—YOU MAKE THE REVISIONS FUN AND I LOOK
FORWARD TO MORE. . .

FOR ALL THOSE WONDERFUL BOOKS I ENJOY READING. . .

MOST OF ALL, GOD FOR MY WRITING AND IN ANSWERING PRAYERS.

FOR MY READERS . . . MAY YOU NEVER STOP DREAMING OR REACHING
FOR A DREAM.

Prologue

Selena Malone sat huddled in a corner, a gun between her knees, ready to protect herself and her team. She needed time to think. Exhaustion had set in from the emotions toiling throughout her mind. Her body needed a release from the pent-up energy of what was to come.

What needed to be done.

She'd seen the warning signs and ignored them. His touch, his smell, his whispered words were so good in a time of darkness. When had she allowed a traitor inside her heart? She didn't have to look at her watch to know she had moments before she would have to run. Her team was in danger, because she had allowed him into heart. And her bed.

When had he turned?

Why had he turned?

Had their love meant anything?

"Selena?"

Damn. She wasn't ready for a lover's lies or confrontations. But she'd learned life did not always give you the time you needed in dealing with the challenges it gave you.

She lifted her head, her hair still covering her face. If he had seen her expression, he would've seen the motto their agents were known for. "Dean."

He was boyishly handsome.

She caught a glimpse of the coolness in his blue eyes, his stance too casual. When he tried too hard to be nonchalant, he was ready to kill.

"Where's your backup?" he asked.

"Does it matter?"

He smiled a lover's smile. "I want my woman protected."

I bet, she thought. "Tell me it's not true."

"What?"

"Dammit, Dean, don't play with me. It's not the day or time," she said, leaning forward, her hair covering the gun and her hands.

He laughed. "Ahhhh ... we can take care of that right here."

First rule of thumb ... Don't patronize a woman.

"They say you're a turncoat," she said, moving her thumb in place.

"I would never turn on my team."

Second rule of thumb ... Don't lie to a woman.

"How else would Donovan's men have known about Sean and Adam? They were undercover for three years, wanting Donovan stopped before any more lives were destroyed. They were within a week of taking Donovan out and he never suspected."

Dean's mouth curved into a lover's smile. "I lost my wife to this job. She didn't like it when I disappeared all the time."

The third, and most important, rule of thumb ... Don't ever use a girl to create a cat fight.

Selena stood up with one jump, her gun at her leg. She approached him with a smile that made promises burn out of control. "What was the last straw in turning?"

She advanced and when she was a kiss away, she stood on her toes, waiting.

"You were the deciding factor."

Her lips touched his. "How?"

"Wouldn't you like to know?" He smiled into the kiss.

She kissed him for old time's sake, feeling nothing but a lover's betrayal. "Not really." She tucked her arm into his chest. "A part of me will miss you, though."

"Miss me? You can't get rid of me. I've been prom— "

He reeled back and blood poured from his head as he went down. It wasn't her shot. She looked around, seeing nothing, hearing nothing. Silencer. The men had promised her she had this

6

one all alone. Who had taken the head shot?

It was time to leave this scene. She needed laughter, a little sunshine, and just plain good folks. Some sense of a normal life before it was too late.

And a decent cup of coffee.

Chapter One

Two years later

Puffs of smoke sailed across the room. Danten paced the floor, rolling the cigar between his thumb and fingers before lifting it to his mouth. He paused.

"Did you find her?" Danten finally asked.

The seasoned investigator, who called himself Jones, waved the smoke away.

"She's covered her trail completely, sir. No credit card, phone, or any other kind of data exists. Even her comrades — "

"Former comrades," Danten said quietly.

"Even they haven't seen her."

"Not that they would want to after her former lover turned against his own team. She had guts wanting to finish him off face-to-face." Danten puffed on his cigar a few more times and went back to rolling it between his fingers, knowing she hadn't pulled the trigger. But then … no one knew who had but him. "When she walked out on the mission, it was the final straw. They could understand being taken in by a lover, but not a comrade leaving them high and dry in a mission." He knew the silent code of honor.

She would be on her own.

Jones stepped forward slightly, hesitating. "Why look her up after all this time?"

"Because she can take care of her sister's debt."

"But you're—"

Danten snuffed out his cigar back and forth with gentle motions. He laid the cigar down and waited. "Do you have any other leads?"

Jones hesitated again. Was he having second thoughts? "No. I'll let you know as soon as I receive any info."

"I see." Danten's eyes narrowed, but he nodded and smiled. As Jones turned away, he asked, "Don't you want your other half of the fee?"

There was the slightest pause, but Jones continued out the door. "No. I can get it when you get the rest of your information."

"Our deal was paid in full regardless of the outcome as long you uncovered every nook and cranny."

"I did."

"I have your money."

Danten had picked the investigator for the greedy soul he possessed. And his refusal of the money meant he was letting his scruples get in the way of doing the job. Danten opened his desk drawer — and in a moment it was over.

Danten didn't wait for the investigator's last breath before reaching inside the man's jacket and pulling out the envelope he found there. He ripped the envelope open. Just as he suspected, Jones had found her.

Sliding the envelope and its contents into his briefcase, he snapped the locks into place. A few well-placed leads under the right noses and he would take it from there.

In time, Selena would pay her sister's debt.

Chapter Two

Drake Carpoli's body hummed with the need to destroy the face etched in his mind, which played the scene over and over, refusing him solitude.

"She couldn't be over fifty-five. Her body hasn't stiffened. Do you see this mark here?" Drake's boss and longtime mentor, Larry White, pointed with the antenna of his ancient cell phone to the two burnt lines on the victim's left shoulder blade.

"Where's the other one?" Drake asked, bending down, his gloved fingers searching for the third mark.

"This is where we're stumped. Normally, and I use the word loosely, the Donovans keep the three marks together as a symbol for anyone thinking of betraying them. Once you're in, you're in. Do you notice where they tossed her?"

Drake didn't give a flying fig where they dumped the bodies. He surveyed the area with disinterest. A rundown shack. Row after row of empty rusty dumpsters needing to be overhauled or crushed waited at the foot of the landfill's foul-smelling heap. If he hadn't woken up with a headache and a stuffy nose, he doubted he'd have stayed here this long. This wasn't his scene. He had been due elsewhere but had heard about the discovery of the burial and decided it was worth a visit. He wasn't a praying man, but he'd prayed every night his brother would be found.

The sound of heavy machinery running at odd hours had awakened one of the transients, and that had gotten the police involved. Now a cadaver dog and his partner were looking for more bodies.

There was no doubt Drake's brother lay under the city's waste.

It was another hour before he was uncovered. Drake had finally taken a cup of black coffee and sat on the hood of the new old beater car he'd recently purchased, refusing to drive his Hummer to places like this.

Drake barely glanced at Jeremy, a young colleague, as the kid walked over to him. He didn't hate the obnoxious pup, but he didn't have to like him either. He raised a brow, waiting.

"They've found your brother." Jeremy tilted his head back. "And your other truck is no longer on the missing list."

Drake threw the half-empty cup onto the already scum-covered ground. "Does he have the marks?" he ground out.

"You'd better look for yourself."

His back towards Larry and Jeremy, Drake stood at the edge of the hole, immobile, staring at his kid brother's body. The fact his brother had been buried in this rotting wasteland didn't ignite the rage as much seeing his body decomposing, naked, gelded and labeled a traitor — Donovan style.

Drake strode past them, then spun around with a right cross and decked Jeremy.

"What the hell was that for?" Jeremy asked.

"You explain it to him," Drake told Larry and walked away.

Chapter Three

Selena fingered the cross around her neck. She didn't bother locking the door behind her.

There wasn't a care in the world in this small town called Heaven's Way, Ohio. There wasn't a need to lock doors or cars. The crime rate was almost zilch. The town was aptly named and the people within the community played a great part in keeping its name accurate. She pushed open the gate and cringed when it slammed behind her. She had forgotten it was still five in the morning. She started down the sidewalk. Her cell phone vibrated.

The illumination read *unknown caller.*

Normally, the only people who had her number didn't block their number. Her past certainly didn't have her number. And if it had found her, she wasn't answering.

The phone vibrated again.

She ignored it.

It vibrated again.

Gut instinct said her past had caught up with her.

But why?

She wasn't sure if she wanted to know. Her judgment — her misjudgment — had altered the lives of the families of the men who had died because she'd trusted Dean. She'd allowed herself to get close to him, leading him to the heart of their mission — all because she had fallen for the illusion of love and a shoulder to lean on. She'd walked away after he was killed, knowing she'd let her comrades down. The doubts of trusting her own comrades when greed could motivate the strongest man and woman were too hard to ignore. When she'd given her resignation, she'd hoped it wasn't too late to live again.

Every day here meant she could enjoy life from the inside out. A chance at a normal life.

Still, at times, she found herself wondering about the what ifs and who had closed the door for Dean.

No one could ever change the past. And if she could've, she always wondered if she would've.

There was one problem.

In order to think properly, she had needed her one and only love in life.

Coffee.

She had about died when she realized there wasn't one coffee house in Heaven's Way. Within a year she had changed that, opening Heaven's Brew. By the time summer had arrived, an indoor-outdoor garden patio in the rear had been constructed and she had added a retractable awning and tables in the front. She had forced the past behind her, forgetting the games of the Agency, reminding herself that life was not all made of lies and betrayals. By the time opening day had come and gone, the people of Heaven's Way had seen a side of her she had forgotten existed.

It was a side of her she liked. And wanted to keep.

This time the vibration was short and sweet. A text message had been sent to her.

She sighed, flipped open the phone and clicked to read the text. It was short and sweet—just like the sender.

Answer the phone.

Another text popped in. She clicked on it and grinned.

Quit smiling.

This time when the phone vibrated, she answered, "Hello?"

"Selena? It's Martha."

Her friend. And her ex-boss' wife.

"Hi, Martha. How are you?" Selena asked, not quite sure of the reception since she'd bowed out of the last mission, leaving her comrades with one less man and without a replacement for her.

"Listen. I understand why you left when you did. I haven't gotten in touch because if Larry even thought for one sweet second I was thinking of calling you ..." Martha's voice trailed off.

That meant Larry was close by and Martha didn't have much time.

"Yesterday, Larry received a call and your name came out. I hadn't heard him say it since the day you left."

"I know he was mad — I'm sorry I left the way I did. I had to — "

"They took our daughter."

"*What?*" Selena stopped walking, rooted. "Lacey? They took Lacey? I didn't know—I would never have left without making sure Lacey was back in your arms." And she wouldn't have left another woman with the uncertainty of not knowing whether her daughter was alive or dead.

Or worse. Sold into the Donovans' slave market. The slavery ring Selena had been investigating before Dean had betrayed her and she'd quit the Agency.

Martha's voice changed abruptly. Larry must have appeared. "I'm sorry. I have no comment. There's no word on our daughter and there are other families you can do articles on. I don't want to discuss it."

The phone went dead. And so did the rest of whatever warning Martha had been relaying.

Selena's heart ached for Martha and Larry. If she had not abandoned the mission, maybe Lacey would not have been abducted. Lacey's disappearance renewed Selena's own heartache for her missing stepsister, Theresa. It had been almost three years since she had seen or heard from Theresa.

She wished she still had her contacts, but since she had bowed out of the mission at such a crucial time, she had been blackballed. The only resources left were talking with the authorities, filing missing reports and offering a reward for her safe return or information leading to Theresa.

Martha must have used her own connections in finding Selena, because Selena had covered her tracks well. Even after thirty-five years of marriage, Larry still didn't know everything about Martha. Deep in thought, Selena walked by her neighbor's house and the front door opened. Mrs. Irons poked her head out.

"Selena, if you'll wait a moment, I'd like to walk with you."

Young and old called the elderly woman "Mrs. Irons." No one knew her first name and those who dared to inquire for one were shot down with a smile and a pat on the cheek. Mrs. Irons wore her silver hair straight. She wrapped a matching silver shawl around her shoulders as she joined Selena on the sidewalk, her tennis shoes silent.

"Do you remember the cabin in the valley?" Mrs. Irons asked.

"I remember."

"Well … Mary Ann Jenkins at Jenkins Realty mentioned she'd just sold the place to an anonymous buyer who happened to find a renter for the summer. Mary Ann let it slip by accident, mind you." Mrs. Irons winked. "I'd heard the renter was unattached. Of course, there are many unattached men in this town. Though I have to say you're going about it the right way. Why, these young girls chasing after the boys, calling them up, asking them for a date—that isn't the way to go. Men love a challenge. The hunt. My mother taught me a lady should know what she wants and who she wants … Just don't show it. Let him think it's his idea."

Selena knew she would be the talk of the town until someone new came into the area. Now they could work their matchmaking skills on him.

Just not with her.

They had reached Heaven's Brew. "Mrs. Irons, would you like a cup of coffee? I'd love it if you could join me. My treat," Selena offered, finding the key to her shop and opening it up.

Mrs. Irons shook her head. "I wish I could, dearie, but I must get back to Duke. He misses me when I'm not there."

"Mrs. Irons, if I may ask …What did you do before you retired here?"

"I guess you could say communications. Why do you ask?"

Selena really couldn't say why she asked. "Curiosity, I guess."

"I can relate very well to that. I like your directness. Someday soon we'll sit and have a chat about it. Gotta go." Mrs. Irons sprinted off. Duke, her dog, probably didn't require as much attention as she seemed to think, but Selena didn't comment. It never failed to amaze Selena to see Mrs. Irons take off like that. She knew many people over the age of seventy jogged, but the speed Mrs. Irons could obtain was amazing.

From the time the first customer came in until the lull before lunch, she wasn't able to give Martha's call a thought. Part of her hadn't really wanted to dwell on it too much, knowing she wasn't going to like finding out why Larry had been talking about her.

One of the girls behind the counter came out and handed Selena an order, nodding towards the door.

Selena was way ahead of her.

The towns' matrons had tried to set her up with every single man in town, including the hapless Tom, so now Selena's radar now went off way before any of the men entered the building. It wasn't that the guys weren't kindhearted or handsome, but she wanted to enjoy life without the complications of dating.

Tom waved.

"Hi, Tom. The usual?" Selena called out.

Selena didn't hold it against him or the others when they placed bets to see who she'd go out with. It was part of the male species. She'd seen it many times with her work colleagues.

She made Tom's drink and took it over to him. "I hear you're dating Patti these days. She's a great lady." She didn't wait around for Tom's answer. Whether Tom admitted it or not, Patti and he made a great couple.

On her way back to the counter, she noticed a man in the corner, quietly observing Tom and his buddies.

She had first noticed the stranger several weeks ago. He came in early every day, working on his laptop. She couldn't help notice how his jeans emphasized every little detail all the way up to his lean hips to his black T-shirt. She had a feeling he could handle himself in any situation.

He never said much in the way of the words, but his silver blue eyes had no trouble conveying he liked what he saw.

Her body was a traitor, forgetting her rule of not getting involved whenever his silver blue eyes told her he wanted her. His hands on the coffee mug seemed to add a subtle intent to caress her body soon.

In his own time.

She had forgotten what it was like to feel, to be caressed, to whisper the heat into flames, but she couldn't allow it to happen. The past was not so buried she couldn't remember what it had cost her and the other families.

A small bell clanked as Patti walked in.

Tom shifted towards the exit. "I have to get going. Got an appointment."

"I'll tag along," Patti said, coming up beside him. She latched onto Tom's arm and walked out with him.

Tom's face turned beet red. He didn't pull away from her, though, when she kissed his cheek.

Selena turned towards the stranger. "They make a great couple," she said as Tom and Patti left.

The stranger studied his cup through hooded eyes. "It's not going to work."

She faced him, puzzled. "What's not going to work?"

The stranger regarded her with wry amusement. "Distractions. By the way, the name's Drake Carpoli."

Chapter Four

Drake didn't have to like the fact Larry White had forced him to take a sabbatical for decking Jeremy.

He hadn't had to like it, but he'd accepted it, especially when Larry had put it to him the way he had: "Get your head on straight or lose the job."

Drake reached into the ice chest and pulled out a frosted beer.

His phone vibrated. Larry.

He answered his boss' call by asking, "When are you going to get a real refrigerator?"

"I just bought the damn place. Consider yourself lucky it was there for you to take your vacation."

"Don't you mean forced leave of absence? Because it sure as hell wasn't voluntary."

"You know... I might join you and check out the area. Anything interesting pop up?"

Drake walked out to the front porch, which had a spectacular view of the town. The only thing he had found interesting was a woman named Selena. "Didn't you check out the area? You bought this place sight unseen? That's not like you, White. What are you up to?"

"I surf the net once in awhile." This brought laughter from Drake. Everyone knew Larry hated technology. "Martha's always trying to get me to take a vacation. I had one of the girls do a little searching. They showed me some pictures and I thought Martha would enjoy it."

Drake sat in the chair made from logs. "That explains why it's so rustic. Nothing has Martha's touch. Which means, Larry, you're not only up to something, but if Martha finds out, you're dead. And I'll help her kill you."

"Repeat that. You're breaking up. I'm losing you."

The line went dead. Larry's way of avoidance.

Drake leaned against the wall and propped his feet up. He closed his phone and inserted it back onto his belt. It was too quiet here. When he had seen the location of Larry's cabin, he was ready to turn and go back, no matter what the consequences. He couldn't retire from the agency. The clawing need for revenge against the Donovans for killing his brother had taken over every part of his life. His only agenda was getting through this enforced leave to take them out.

Thankfully, he'd smuggled the Donovan reports from his desk for late night reading to ferret out any new leads on Donovan's weaknesses, anything that might lead him to Donovan's next move. Except thoughts of Selena interrupted his flow of concentration.

He hadn't scouted the outside of the cabin earlier and now was as good a time as any to get his focus back on track. A map of the few manmade trails in the wooded area had been taped inside the cabinet door above the sink, marking locations of stores, residential homes, and other trails within the area.

An ax butted against a stump and logs were stacked three feet high under a tarp. The wood bin overflowed with seasoned wood and kindling had been thrown in a crate next to it. Because of the pine trees blocking the sun, there were more patches of sandy dirt than grass. He'd almost forgotten how sweet the scent of pine trees smelled. His world had always left a foul scent in the wake of its violence. Even in silence, the guns and impending danger had overwhelmed the silence, unable to give the agents time to completely regenerate for the next day.

A branch snapped in the woods.

Drake waited.

Nothing came into sight.

"Are you Drake Malone?" a woman asked.

He turned, wary. She had appeared out of nowhere. He sighed. Too much of the past was hard to get out of his system.

"Selena thought you might need a few provisions until you get stocked up." She held up a basket of muffins and a covered dish.

The food smelled delicious. "Why didn't she bring them up herself?" he asked, offering to take them from her. The covered dish was spaghetti, homemade meatballs, and sauce.

The girl was very pretty, wearing no makeup and dressed for hiking.

"Oh, Selena didn't make these. I did. She thought you wouldn't know many people since you're new and all and thought you might like some company."

Was Selena matchmaking? The girl followed him inside the cabin, not waiting on ceremony.

"Great place," she said. "We wondered who would buy this place. It's a bit of a fetch from here to town, but you look in great shape and can probably handle it."

His eyebrow rose.

"You seem to know my name," he said.

"Oh. Sorry. Name's Katrina Belford. I'm your neighbor." She grinned and held out her hand as he grinned back. "Around these parts, a neighbor up here can be as far as a few miles away."

As politely as he could, he ushered Katrina out the door, but not before she reached up and hugged him.

He froze.

"Selena did the same thing when I hugged her." Katrina seemed puzzled. "Come to think of it ... Mrs. Irons did the same thing. I guess you'll all get used to it. We're huggy around here." She laughed at his expression. "Not the men. Don't worry." Katrina waved and headed outside, her ponytail bouncing with each step.

He watched Katrina as she took the road into town. Not a twinge of spark when Katrina hugged him. He knew he didn't have to hug Selena to know what he would feel for her.

Flipping open his laptop, he began surfing the marked pages he still had access to. Two hours later, phone calls and surfing results brought nothing in new leads on the Donovans' activities.

He leaned back in his chair and propped his feet on the desk, crossing them over each other. Selena hadn't left his thoughts completely. The silent sparring, his body going into overdrive, Selena's attitude all added up to one thing. He wanted her. If he didn't convince her they would be good together, she would continue sending distractions his way. He pulled his feet from the desk. One day was one day too long in putting Selena's matchmaking on ice.

He locked the doors and almost ran into a woman carrying jugs of what looked like apple cider.

She smiled. "Hi. I'm Sandy Kitt from the apple orchard on the other side of your trails." At the lift of his eyebrow, she added, "The trail behind your place leads to mine. I thought I'd bring over some apple cider until you had a chance to stock up the place."

Drake couldn't help but laugh. "Let me guess. Selena?"

"Why ... yes." She handed him the cider after he unlocked the door and gestured for her to follow him in.

Placing the cider in the ice chest, he decided he would have to buy Larry a refrigerator or he'd never fit any meat in here. After they spoke a few minutes, Sandy took off — not before she gave him a hug and kiss on the cheek.

He quickly changed into jogging clothes in case Selena sent anyone else over. He could use jogging as an excuse to keep on the move.

Within twenty minutes he was standing in front of Heaven's Brew. He walked in and found her congregating with five women, two of whom he had just met. All six were huddled and whispering.

He walked by the group. "Hello, ladies." He ordered a caramel latte. The whipped cream and chocolate fudge drizzle oozed out of the lid. Selena's favorite. He walked over to the guys standing by the counter. He'd met Tom, Henry, and John on previous visits to the coffee shop.

"Don't worry. You guys are out of the loop on this one," Drake remarked dryly. "It seems I'm her next target."

"What happened? Food delivery?"

"Apple cider?"

"Massage?"

Drake, Tom, and Henry turned. "Massage?"

A flush crept up John's face. "Well, I'd just gotten out of the shower and when I walked into the living room, Cassie had set her equipment up. The next thing I know, her hands are all over me. So how could I say no?"

"Say *no*," they chorused.

"Easy for you guys to say. It's not the beginning campaign you have to worry about. She just wears you down with the first group and after that it's too late," Henry said into his coffee cup. "Look out, here she comes." He left the counter.

Selena brought an empty cup and filled it for Drake. Her eyes sparkled with mischief. "Had a chance to meet your neighbors yet?"

"You know I have. You sent them over," he whispered, leaning toward her.

"There are plenty of people to meet. Enjoy your stay."

His hand prevented her escape.

He could feel her struggle for domination over her emotions.

"This is for you." He held out the coffee he'd ordered. "No?"

Still holding her, he circled the cup within an inch of her mouth. He knew the combination was irresistible. When she looked at him, he saw the unspoken words that said he wasn't playing fair.

He brought it back to him and licked the sauce from the lid. "Delicious."

She pulled away. Foreplay with coffee was a new approach.

He lifted the cup in the air as a salute and walked out, whistling.

*

Selena didn't stop until she had walked out into the alley.

Closing her eyes, she leaned against the double doors, finding it hard to battle her attraction for this man. Instead, she focused on something less pleasant: how she had failed so many people by allowing Dean into her heart.

How could she ever explain that to them? That she had caved for a shoulder to lean on, to cry on and to be held during those dark times? Until Drake, she hadn't missed those feelings.

It was the slightest sound, but she'd heard him.

A shadow crossed the toe of her shoe.

She followed the trail up and met Drake's scrutiny head on, daring him to cross the line.

He not only dared, he walked straight up to her, pulled her into his arms, and gave her a taste of what he'd offered earlier. He kissed her like a drowning man in a sea of darkness, reaching for the light. Reaching for hope. Desire mixed with cream, caramel, and chocolate.

And heaven.

He slowly released her.

"Chocolate, caramel, and whipped cream make a powerful combination. I found it hard not to share."

She pushed him away, frustrated with her self-imposed roadblocks and for him reading her mind and her body.

"How long are you staying?" Hand on the doorknob, she turned it slowly and opened it, ready to escape the truth.

He placed a hand above her head and closed the door gently. "I'm not sure. It depends on you."

She didn't dare turn in case he saw the tears.

Or the aftereffects of his kiss.

Chapter Five

The next morning was too busy for her to spend too much time thinking about Drake. When the phone rang, she darted into the backroom to pick it up.

"Heaven's Brew."

She heard her investigator's voice and gripped the phone tighter.

"Selena, I've run down those leads we discussed—nothing. They're all dead ends."

"What about that woman in Springfield?"

"Turns out she tips off the police about five times a week. Another crank."

God help her. It was worse than she'd thought.

"There have to be more people you can talk to — "

"I'm sorry, Selena. There's nothing."

"People can't just disappear like that!"

But Selena knew they could.

"I'm sorry," he said again, and she knew he meant it.

Her hands shook as she hung up the phone. She grabbed her coat. It was impossible to focus on conversation or the smallest of details, such as brewing coffee, at this time. "I'm leaving. I'll be back before the end of the shift," she told her helper.

She hardly noticed the walk home. Her hand shook as she fumbled for the key, making several attempts in fitting it into the lock. She opened the door and walked as far as the stairway and held onto to the banister. Unable to focus or feel, she sat down.

She folded her arms over her bent knees, buried her face and gave into the grief she'd been holding back, letting go of the hope of ever finding her sister alive.

Of ever finding answers.

A cold nose nudged her arms. Duke pushed his head through her barrier and licked her face. She wasn't sure how long she had cried, but she couldn't stop. She held onto Duke's neck, her tears falling on his thick coat.

Someone gently moved Duke aside and unbuttoned her coat.

She was so tired she couldn't open her eyes, but somehow she knew it was Drake.

He lifted her into his arms and carried her upstairs.

"Where's your bedroom?" he asked.

"Why?" She trusted him but didn't trust her own attractions to him while her barriers were down.

He held her close to him "You need rest." He found her bedroom without her help, laid her on the king-size bed, and opened the chest at the foot of the bed. Pulling a light blanket out, he unfolded it and covered her up.

Selena didn't have the strength to ask him why he was in her house.

*

When she woke up an hour later, Selena saw Drake sprawled in the chair, his eyes closed. Duke crawled up to her and licked her face. She rolled on her side and studied the man edging too close to her heart. Duke nudged her arm with his nose, crawling closer. The man sleeping a few feet away warned her he was going to be a challenge.

Fool that she was, she told herself, rubbing the shepherd's ears, it was better to keep her distance.

Where was her sister?

The feeling of helplessness was too close for comfort. Being in Drake's arms, surrounded by his determination and protection was too close for comfort. Selena pushed the feelings aside, not willing to give into weakness.

She could feel the tears welling up in her eyes and closed her eyes, hoping they would stay hidden. She needed to be alone with her thoughts.

Drake would ask questions when he awakened.

And he would demand answers.

She rolled over to check the clock. It was time to get up. The bed moved again. Thinking it was Duke, she patted the bed only to have her hand enclosed in Drake's.

"What's going on?" Drake wasn't about to compromise.

"Apparently not much with you hovering over me." Attitude leaped where treading lightly in this position should've taken lead. "I appreciate the neighborly gesture earlier. Really sweet, but I can take it from here." She ducked under his arm.

Drake pinned her with his eyes. "Everyone is worried about you. Apparently, it's not like you to take off, leaving Heaven's Brew attended by the others."

His lips were close enough to taste with the tip of her tongue, but it was too dangerous to give into temptation.

He captured her face with the palm of his hand, thumb stroking her cheek. His lips brushed against hers. Testing. When he found no resistance, his hand stroked the inside of her wrist softly. His mouth covered hers.

She sighed. It was fruitless to resist temptation when he was providing the opportunity. The soft gentle persuasion of curiosity and attraction created a hot combination. He pulled her close, wanting more than a kiss.

She returned the kiss and when she realized the door was opening more than she cared, she slid away. He stalled the move and pulled her into his arms, content with holding her.

Duke whined at the doorway, his head moving from the stairs to Drake and Selena. The sound of Mrs. Irons' heavy tread and huffing and puffing alerted them to her arrival.

"In my day and age, the youngsters came to the elderly. With my hips and knees, it's a wonder I've made it this far."

Selena placed a hand on Drake's shoulder. She shook her head and whispered, "You're new here. And because your kiss is passable, I'll fill you in." She simply smiled at the male affronted look, showing him she was giving him a hard time. "Mrs. Irons can run faster than I can and she can jump the gate at her place."

Mrs. Irons popped her head in as Drake moved around the bed. "Everything going okay? Drake, would you be a dear and run downstairs? Selena and I have to do some girly chitchat. Thank you." Straight and to the point Mrs. Irons was. "We'll be down in a few minutes." Mrs. Irons dismissed Drake affectionately, but meaningfully. She waited until Drake left the room, then sat down, patting the bed with her cane.

Now when did Mrs. Irons start using a cane? Selena sat on the edge of the bed. "Mrs. Irons, I know how to handle myself—"

Mrs. Irons bowed her head and sighed. "No, dear, we're not having the birds and the bees talk. I think of you as another daughter, but I barely got through that time period with my own. I don't think I can go through it again." She reached over and patted Selena's knee. "It's another talk I have in mind. I have never seen you cry before. I want to help if I can."

Selena pushed the creeping sadness back down into the depths of her heart. She didn't want to start crying again.

"There's nothing you can do. I've exhausted all my connections in finding leads to my sister." Selena couldn't sit any longer and began pacing. "Every time I think I've found a link, it fizzles."

Mrs. Irons leaned onto her cane, the motions of her hands the same as one would a worry stone. "I have a few connections from my own past. Let me help."

"I don't have much hope."

Mrs. Irons stood with the aid of her cane, a determined look on her face. "I have a group of women friends who specialize in networking. Let me see what I can come up with. Jot down the specifics of your sister and locate a photo and we'll go from there. It doesn't hurt to keep trying. Does it?" She patted Selena on the shoulder. "This one isn't going to be as easy to rid of as the others. Is he?" And winked as she left the room.

Chapter Six

Drake was sitting at the table in the kitchen with Mrs. Irons, waiting for Selena to come downstairs. He was itching to find out what had caused Selena's upset, but Mrs. Irons wouldn't say anything.

Selena finally came into the room, looking distressed but determined. She handed over a folder and a photo to Mrs. Irons.

No one objected when Drake studied the photo. The girl was waif-like in face and body. Straight blonde hair. Her eyes didn't quite meet the camera. Very shy. She did not resemble dark-haired Selena in the least.

"Who is she?"

Selena poured a cup of coffee and sat at the table. "My stepsister. Theresa was known for her whirlwind relationships, keeping everyone in the dark. So when I received a wedding invitation by voicemail, I wasn't surprised. She said she would introduce us and tell us all about him when we arrived. My job wouldn't allow time off for the wedding and when I had missed it, she stopped answering my calls. Her phone number was disconnected. Mail came back 'addressee unknown.' I went to the last address she had given us, only to find a couple who had lived there for the past twenty years. I checked property tax and deed records. Nothing."

"Is what why you were so upset today?"

"Yes. I hired an investigator to follow up some leads. He had some bad news."

Drake could tell how difficult this was for her from the way her voice shook.

"And Mrs. Irons says she has some old friends who might be able to help." Selena indicated the envelope and the photo.

"Where are your parents?" Drake felt for Selena. She shouldn't have to do this on her own.

Duke pushed his nose on Selena's lap and whined. She rubbed Duke's ears. "A few months before Theresa's wedding, my parents decided to follow up on a real estate lead in Barbados when their plane went down. Their bodies and plane were never recovered."

She added apologetically, "I really need to get back to the shop and close up." She kissed Duke on the snout.

"Come on, Duke. We have a mission to complete." Mrs. Irons waved and was out the door without the aid of her cane.

"I'll walk with you," Drake said to Selena.

"I'm okay now. The last straw was hearing I'd hit another dead end. But I'm not giving up until I can hear her voice." She locked the front door behind them. "And put whoever kidnapped her behind bars."

He walked beside her, matching stride easily. "I know how you feel."

She shot him a glance that told him she didn't think so.

"Someone killed my brother during an assignment he was on. I intend to make sure his murderer is dealt with."

"Oh God, Drake. I'm so sorry. What happened?"

"I was sent a message." Drake stepped off the sidewalk, taking Selena with him as a couple of kids rode past them on bikes. "A video accompanied the message, giving a second by second account of the torture and burial. We analyzed the background noise and scenery to find the location of his body."

"I am so sorry."

"He was found dead, buried in the city trash heap. The hardest part was telling my parents." They were in front of the coffee shop. "Listen, maybe my contacts can help you. At least I know my brother's dead, but you're hanging out there. Let me help."

She looked up at him. "I don't know what you could do about any of it."

"I know some investigators."

She hesitated, then nodded. "I'll find another picture and write down the information."

"I'll pick you up for dinner later," he said. "We can talk about it more then."

She looked like she was struggling, wanting to say no.

"I really think I can help, Selena," he said.

"All right," she said. "Seven o'clock."

"Seven o'clock," he said, and resisted the temptation to kiss her again.

*

"Why did you move here?" Selena asked that evening when Drake came to pick her up for dinner, sliding into the car on the passenger side.

"Why not here?" he countered, smoothly putting the car into drive and heading into town.

She positioned herself to see him better. "Come on. A few weeks ago you were bored out of your mind, wondering what the hell brought you here. And because you would never have chosen this area to take a break. You look like the type who would've worked until retirement, skipping all vacations because no one would do the job to suit you."

"My boss suggested I take a vacation."

"You were ordered to take a leave of absence?"

He laughed. "You could say that. Why didn't you ever give those guys a chance?"

She could tell he was trying to change the subject. "I'm not into dating."

"They would've bored you to death."

"Yes. I mean no. They were nice, expecting the homey atmosphere of a cooked meal every night. And that's not me." She slipped her hair behind her ear for a better view of him. "I didn't even know a person could use browned bananas until Mrs. Irons baked some banana bread with them. I get by, but I don't think they'd have appreciated the lack of talents in that area." Hand under her chin, she stared out the window.

"That explains the attitude. You're not eating enough." His tone wry. "You're not a morning person until you've had your coffee, either."

"When I moved here, the first thing I craved was gourmet coffee. I had developed a habit I couldn't do without. The need for coffee. Strong, silent, and kick-ass. The closest thing I found was in the grocery store, and if I doubled the suggested amount, I was able to achieve the wide-eyed look, but my senses still weren't satisfied. I wanted to smell the richness, feel the strength in the first sip, and by the end of the day still ready to kick ass if I had to. Though my attitude is from the past, I've hung onto it just in case."

"Don't your senses miss anything else?" he asked.

Her eyebrow rose. "You mean sex, don't you?"

The half-smile on his face told her he did.

"The wild emotions that come within relationships—with sex—don't fit into my life right now," she said.

He drove into the paved circular drive of Maurice's, a well-known surf-and-turf restaurant, and parked. The valet opened his door and another waited to help her out, but Drake gestured he'd do it. She'd hesitated when he offered to help her out of the car, knowing his touch would send her heart racing—and it did.

"A penny for your thoughts," she said, once seated.

"I'll share mine for free," he leaned over, whispering them from behind.

Her breath hitched. "I'll keep mine to myself."

He sat down and picked up the wine list, gesturing for her to choose. She shook her head and suggested he do it. "That sounds like a challenge."

"It's not. It's a choice."

He gave his selection for the house wine to the waiter, who then handed them each a menu.

Selena chose oysters and a salad. Drake's eyes widened at her selection. She blushed. Drake ordered the prime rib rare and hesitated.

At his hesitation, Selena glanced down at the menu and nodded. "I believe he would like the horseradish."

The waiter accepted their menus, kept his opinions to himself, and disappeared.

"I like the flavor. You don't mind the bite in it?"

She raised her glass of water to him in a small salute. "It's not as if we're going to kiss later. So ... no. But I do like things with a kick to it." She took a small sip, hiding her smile. No doubt he'd take that as a challenge.

"The night is young. You might change your mind. Women have been known to do that."

She laughed.

Music filtered from a shimmering curtain in the corner. The soulful notes drew couples onto the floor and into each other's arms. Lights dimmed above. Candles flickered with enchantment, dancing to notes only lovers could hear.

Selena loved the place. Once in a great while, she and the girls took a night out and relaxed, choosing this place for its quiet atmosphere and fireplaces, totally eliminating the stress and worry from their days.

A hand on her shoulder made her realize how quickly he moved. She didn't question it as he held out his hand and placed her hand into his, captivated by the silent amusement and heat in his eyes.

He led her onto the dance floor, the spot secluded and dark. His arms surrounded her, drawing her close. She could handle this.

For the moment.

His fingers caressed her back, reminding her of the same circular motions he'd made on his cup. The same silent promise in his eyes. Her nipples tightened at the thought of his hands, his mouth, caressing her. The way he kissed already spelled trouble.

"What are you thinking?" he asked softly.

The sensations he was creating had lulled her into contentment.

"Nothing."

He placed her hand on his shoulder and lifted her chin. "Nothing, huh? You're not a very good liar."

He brushed a gentle kiss on her lips. Surrender came easily, her lips parting for more. He enfolded her hand back in his. "I'll wait for another time and place to finish this."

She sighed. She was breaking her rule of no dating. Not wanting to give into the emotions spiraling inside but knowing she would surrender if her plan to match him up with someone else didn't work fast enough. If it did work, she wasn't so sure she could stand watching him with another woman.

After the last note faded into the shadows, he held her hand, refusing to surrender it as they walked back to the table.

"How long are you staying?" she asked. She missed the warmth of his embrace and caresses. Not a good sign in her book.

"For a few weeks. Are you ready for me to leave so soon?"

"I was wondering who I should send next."

Nothing like placing all the cards on the table.

His eyes narrowed. "Sweetheart, you can send all the women you want, but it won't work. When I make up my mind, nothing can deter me. If you want to ignore what's between us, I can wait. But not in the background."

Chapter Seven

Selena was disappointed he hadn't kissed her when he walked her to the front door and left as she walked inside. The meal was delicious and their camaraderie was contagious with the playful bantering. Every time she asked him a question, he'd answered with half answers. He reminded her of the Agency.

She pushed the door open and found the lights had been turned off. She flipped the switch.

No lights.

She went inside and found the fuse box paneled on the staircase wall. She opened the wood panel and began flipping the switches. Still nothing. She needed a flashlight, which meant she would have to find her way into the kitchen. Her fingers crossed over the banister post and the floor lamp as she made her way across the room.

A floorboard creaked in the hall.

She darted into the kitchen, backing as close as she could into the shadows. Her heel bumped against someone's shoe.

Someone grabbed her from behind. She jabbed with her elbow but was prevented from connecting. A hand secured her against a male body, his grip steel-like, yet surprisingly gentle. She struggled to find an opening.

Another hand secured her head back, muffling her screams.

"Listen, Selena. There's someone in the house. I remembered you left the light on in the kitchen when I'd picked you up. I noticed the lights were all out. Even the outside lamp. Now hold still," Drake warned, removing his hand.

She stepped away but realized he hadn't let go.

"Do you mind?" she whispered. She pulled at his hands, wanting to go after whoever the hell had invaded her home. He

34

released her reluctantly.

The door slammed in the other room. She went after the intruder. Drake's arm snaked out to stop her and reeled her back. She dodged and raced after the intruder. He touched her shoulder. She grabbed his hand and him over her shoulder, landing him flat on his back.

"Dammit, Drake. I can handle myself," she whispered.

Amusement glinted in his smile. "I can see that. Remind me never to tick you off. I'd like to know where you learned krav."

Still hot at missing the intruder, she sat on him before he could get up. "I'll give you some advice, honey. I've been a black belt for seven years and can flip you any time I want. So that you understand something else, any time you want to see how far you can push my buttons, remember you have a few of your own."

He didn't challenge her. "Let's check out the house," he suggested.

She gave him one of the flashlights that she kept in the kitchen, using the other herself. A thorough search turned up nothing about the intruder or a solution to her electrical problems.

"Where's your key?" Drake asked.

She handed it to him and located her cell phone, searching for Tom's number. Hopefully, she wouldn't be killed for calling this late.

"Who are you calling?"

She looked up. "Tom. He's the town's electrician."

He closed her phone. "It's too dark to check it out now. We'll do it tomorrow. In the meantime, you can stay with me."

"I'll call Mrs. Iron. She has a spare room."

"The only light on in Mrs. Irons' house is a small nightlight in the kitchen. She's probably asleep. I won't touch you if you don't want to be touched. I'll respect your wishes. And your space." He ushered her out the door, locking it behind them. "But if you give me an indication it's a go, then there are no holds barred."

"Remember I can take care of myself."

"Oh, I'll remember not to underestimate you."

He tucked Selena into the front seat, then paused.

"What did you see?" She'd seen the slight averting of his gaze.

"Probably a cat, but I want to check it out. Stay here."

She stayed, but she didn't like it. He was back a few moments later.

"What was it?" she asked.

"I saw a couple of shadows running that way." He waved his hand. "Too dark to recognize them, and I didn't want to chase after them with you sitting out here alone."

She didn't want to feel protected, but it was nice to think that for once, someone cared about keeping her safe.

*

After Selena had fallen asleep, Drake sat down on the end of the couch, drawing her feet onto his lap. Her feet were delicate for a woman who could flip him, and his heart, over. He had no doubts these same delicate boned feet were deadly. He stared into the fire. It had been a long time since he'd felt the urges of wanting a home life, a life other than the Agency. There had been other women. They'd understood the lifestyle of the Agency and were well-seasoned agents, but they lacked humor in their determination, having drawn the cold of darkness into their souls to harden them from the danger. Selena's teasing smile and playful matchmaking made it easier for him to forget the darkness.

But he couldn't settle down until he could lay his brother's murderer in the ground where he belonged. If he had his way, that was where he'd put the whole Donovan family.

He laid her feet to the side gently and tended the fire, putting the screen in place. Then he returned to the sofa and reached under her, lifting her head so that he could hold her. She snuggled into his arms easily, wrapping her arms around him. She murmured something about going to bed, wanting to stretch out.

"Are you sure?" he asked.

She nodded.

He carried her into the bedroom and slipped her under the covers. "Where will you sleep?" Her words were whispers, reaching out to him.

He knew where he wanted to sleep, but his mother had taught him to be a gentleman. "On the couch."

But it didn't take long tossing and turning on the couch before he realized there was no getting around it. He wanted in his bed with his arms wrapped around her. It had been a helluva long time since he'd indulged himself in feeling with his body and his emotions. Somehow she'd been able to make him forget what no one else could.

His brother's death.

But he couldn't be swayed from what needed to be done— not even by Selena. Andrew Donovan would pay for what he'd done. There wasn't enough justice in this world for the deaths the Donovan family had ordered. How many families lay awake at night, wondering where their daughters, wives, granddaughters, and nieces were? How many wanted to deliver the same kind of revenge?

Drake felt the shift in the room.

Footsteps that had been trained to be silent. Whoever it was blocked the warmth of the fire.

He had been thinking of Selena and now he was caught unaware.

And without his gun.

If he dropped off the couch or vaulted over the back, his head was an easy mark for their purposes —

"I know you're not asleep."

Selena.

He was going to turn her over his knee for scaring the hell out of him. How had she gotten by him? He let his arm drop slowly, rolling to see her kneeling before the fire, staring at the flames licking the last of the wood.

"You don't say?" he drawled, taken in by the way her dress hugged her hips. The goosebumps on her legs weren't a good sign.

"You're cold. I have some sweats you could change into."

"A six-foot-three man tossing on a couch is a good indication he's not sleeping. And thanks, but no thanks, on the sweats. I really need to check on my house."

Drake's eyes narrowed at the shoes in her hands when she stood.

"Listen. It doesn't matter that this town has to be the most scum-free community I'd ever run across. Someone broke into your home and cut the power and you're not stepping foot out there. Whatever you need will have to be improvised. I'm okay if you want to run around in that sexy dress, wear my sweats, or nothing at all, but you're not leaving until it's daylight."

She turned to leave, but he reached for her arm and held fast.

He read her intentions loud and clear. And had seen the slight movement of her foot, countering it by changing his stance and his distance. Reading the panic in her eyes, he changed tactics. He moved closer, having seen it in some of his comrades' eyes, but he knew if he let her go, he would never forgive himself.

"What do you really need at this moment? And don't tell me clothes or checking on your house. That would be a lie," he said, tipping her chin up in order to get a better look.

She started to shake in his arms.

"Selena…" He was worried as the shakes became uncontrollable in a matter of seconds.

"When I find I've been working too many hours or have been outside very little, I—I—I—This starts. I try so hard to fight it, but I can't seem to shake it. No pun intended," she said with a small laugh. She stiffened her body, trying to control the shakes.

Drake let her go. He was pissed she'd had to go through whatever she had alone. Then or now. He found a large, soft blanket and wrapped it around her.

"Dammit," he ground out, unable to stop worrying when her teeth started chattering so hard he feared she would bit her tongue. He should've recognized the signs. Those goosebumps weren't from the cold but from her inner demons.

He picked her up and cradled her in his arms, holding tight, and headed outside. It was still chilly despite the warmth of the new season. The shaking had subsided to a tiny shiver by the time he'd sat down. He just held her until it was gone. She was so sleepy and worn out from the day, she had trouble keeping her eyes open.

"You're not going back tonight," he said. He kissed her forehead, wishing he could take on the demons. When the time was right, he would ask.

Chapter Eight

Selena didn't know how he'd done it, but he had. Drake had managed to solve the electrical outage at her home, pitched in at Heaven's Brew, and avoided all her matchmaking diversions. In fact, he had managed to turn the tables against her throughout the weeks, convincing the seven diversions she'd sent his way to help him with his plan.

Last week, she had seen Drake and the girls talking at one table and thought she might have succeeded with her diversions. After serving several customers around their table, she noticed they'd stop talking. The girls had the same smiles she was sure she'd worn when her diversions had worked on the other guys.

The bell jingled.

Drake walked in, his face slightly red from jogging in the sun, holding a piece of paper. He waited until she had finished with her customers and asked Josh, one of the high school kids, if he could take over. She thanked Josh and undid her apron.

Drake led her into the back room before he handed her the folded paper. "It's a small lead one of the investigators I told you about found."

She hadn't realized she'd been holding her breath. She turned, not wanting to cry in front of him. He drew her into his arms, giving her support without invading her private thoughts. She was glad he hadn't delivered the information and left. Trembling, she unfolded the paper.

It was an obituary. Her sister's.

Somehow she had known the answer.

Cause of death: natural causes. Private viewing had been for family only. She had been cremated.

Selena needed to get out of here or she would lose it again in front of her staff. And Drake.

"I'm going for a walk," she said.

He followed her out the back entrance, giving no room for her to go alone.

They walked in silence until they were out of town. She couldn't hold back the tears, barely managing to contain the shock.

Her sister had married a man who lived and breathed selling and torturing women. She had never thought for one moment the man her sister married was *the* Donovan.

"This can't be right."

"Why do you say that?"

They reached Drake's cabin. Selena stopped at the edge of the woods behind and looked up at him. "She's never been sick a day in her life. No high blood pressure and shook stress off like a dog does water."

Drake wiped away the tears with his thumb. The palm of his hand cradled the side of her face. "Let's walk," he suggested.

"I know I should feel blessed having this information. And I do. It's just that I feel as if I haven't said my final goodbye. I want to rant and rave at her husband on how selfish he's been, keeping the end of her life to himself. How do you do it? Dealing with your brother's death and not having said good-bye?"

He reached for her hand and she laced her fingers with his. "I don't know. I don't even think how I do it. I've learned life is too short to spend it all grieving, though … I guess patience works wonders." He paused. "I never thought it would happen."

He wasn't talking about his brother. Somehow he'd slipped their relationship in the conversation. If the way he was looking at her now matched how she was feeling, her days in matchmaking were over.

"Oh … hell," he muttered under his breath and kissed her.

Selena felt the love in the kiss. The tenderness. Hesitant. Seeking. It was up to her to give him the answer he was seeking. Maybe her past was no longer an issue and it was time to take a chance.

She held him back. "I need to tell you something."

"Talking wasn't what I had in mind."

"I love you."

He stared at her, not moving. She wondered if she'd misread his body language and subtle hints.

He swept her up in his arms and hugged her. "It's about damned time. I love you, but waiting for you to say you loved me was killing me. I could see it in your eyes and feel it in your body, but you were denying what was inside of you. I was ready to initiate the diversion ladies' help."

"You wouldn't have."

"I see that look in your eyes. It was there when one of the ladies hugged me at the coffee shop the other day. You have beautiful eyes, honey, but they're very expressive."

"Really? I'll have to remedy that."

She wound her arms around his neck and kissed him, showing him her love was real. Somehow she had lost sight of living her life and Drake had shown her it was okay to trust one's heart and give in to love.

"Selena, this isn't the most romantic way in asking ... Will you marry me?"

She buried her head into his neck and sighed.

He tensed.

It wasn't too hard to figure out he was worried she would retract her love as much as she'd sidestepped it. She knew without a doubt he was the one she wanted forever. She just didn't think he wanted all of his questions answered today.

"Yes."

He relaxed. In two seconds, he was carrying her, striding towards the cabin. She knew what his intentions were, but they were going to have another talk.

One he wouldn't like.

Chapter Nine

"Drake…"

How does one tell a man what he wants is not what he's getting?

"What?" His tone was wary.

"We need to talk."

"Later."

"I want to wait until our honeymoon."

He stopped dead in his tracks and met the determination in her eyes.

"You're serious?" He must have read the answer in her eyes. "Damn. You are serious. Cold showers and jogging."

She trailed her fingers down the side of his face to his chest in a light-hearted sensual caress. "Half the fun is getting to that night," she said.

He gently latched onto her fingers and placed a kiss on each tip. "Just so you know… this will be the shortest engagement." He carried her into the cabin, reluctantly putting her down when they were inside.

"Since I've been banned from going into a certain direction, and not that I mind, because I like challenges as much as the next person—" he drawled.

"Don't you mean as much as the next *guy*?" she asked, raiding his cupboards for a snack. "What are you cooking for dinner?" When he didn't answer, she turned around.

He was leaning against the counter, studying her. "Come here."

"Uh-uh." She pivoted smoothly towards the refrigerator, hoping to stall him. He wouldn't force her, but those lips and hands sure could change that *no* to a *yes*.

He reluctantly moved away. "I need to start dinner before we start something else. If you'll find some music and pick out a bottle of wine, I'll do the rest."

He grabbed the pizza dough and poured olive oil on his hands, imagining her lying on the floor as he massaged every inch of that beautiful body. With slow, caressing movements, he worked the dough, pushing and massaging.

A hiss came from her lips.

He moved to the fireplace. He set the grill over the flames, then came back into the kitchen for the dough, carried it to the grill and arranged it carefully.

She moved behind him.

"Honey, you won't be able to put the fire out," he warned, his voice thick with need.

Her hands kneaded his shoulders, gliding to his torso and down his lean abs. She slipped her fingers between skin and the belt area of his jeans, stroking. Her fingers delved lower.

Someone knocked on the door.

She leaned into him, molding her body against him. "Expecting someone?"

"About damn time," he muttered. He wiped his hands on the towel and pulled her hands away. He kissed her gently. "I made plans to help you realize how much you loved me."

Even though Drake didn't show it, Selena knew he was having difficulty in maintaining. She had almost pushed Drake past that point. Part of her wanted him now instead of waiting. It was not that she was totally against making love before their wedding. She just wanted their night to be very special.

Drake opened the door and stepped back.

"It's about time," Katrina said, handing Drake a container. "That needs the freezer. And fast. It's homemade ice cream." Seeing Selena by the counter, she headed that way.

Drake smiled.

Sandy handed Drake's free hand an apple pie and headed

towards the girls. Drake noticed they were all standing by the counter, chatting. He shut the door with his foot.

"More's coming," Tom said from behind the door.

Sherri, Patti, and Cassie filed in and headed over to the counter. John, Henry, and Tom followed.

John rescued the apple pie. "We agreed guys need to band together. After the text messages the girls were sending back and forth, we knew you were in trouble. Besides ... we've decided it was for the best you ended up with Selena."

Henry and Tom smirked.

Mrs. Irons strode past them, minus her cane. "How in the hell are we supposed to know who won the bet?"

Soon the cabin had filled.

"The shop is cleaned and locked up," Josh yelled over everyone, the other kids from Heaven's Brew following.

Drake walked between the ladies and kissed Selena. "Anything else you need to tell me? Any skeletons in the closet?" he asked.

"No." The past didn't need to be revisited. "You?"

"Other than I've decided to retire? No."

*

Selena sat in front of the mirror, surprised at how fast this had happened.

She only wished her parents were alive to share in her happiness. In the span of two weeks, Drake's parents, Katherine and Harold, had flown in, and Drake had surprised her with his grandmother's ring for her wedding ring. Harold had kindly offered to walk her down the aisle, since her own father couldn't be there. And now it was her wedding day.

"My son is so in love with you. I have never seen him happier." Katherine Carpoli, dressed in a simple, but elegant suit, entered the room. She had taken charge of the wedding plans at the church as soon as she realized Selena preferred directing her attention to

Drake and Heaven's Brew.

"Your son is very persistent," Selena said.

The door opened and the sounds of the organ drifted in.

Harold poked his head around the door. "They're starting."

Selena walked over to Harold and kissed him on the cheek. "I'm ready when you are."

Katherine handed Selena the bouquet of flowers. "I have one piece of advice."

"Don't scare her off, Kate," Harold said, smiling at both women with affection.

"It needs to be said. I know my son, Selena. He is the spitting image of his father. When they want something ... they succeed. They're both stubborn as hell, but you won't find two more loyal, protective, loving men."

Katherine quickly kissed Selena and Harold before leaving.

Selena held onto Harold's arm. "Don't worry. I'm not running away."

Tom walked up to them. "An envelope was delivered with your name on it. We don't know who left it. Where do you want it?"

"On the table by the mirror is fine. I'll read it when I change." It was marked *important*. Nothing was more important than the man standing at the end of this red carpet. "Thanks, Tom," she said.

John and Henry opened the doors while Tom hurried past them to sit down.

Selena held Harold's arm and began walking towards the man she had fallen in love with and would spend forever with. He stood by the pastor, waiting patiently. Or at least everyone would think so, but the storm in his blue eyes told her he had waited long enough in igniting the passion between them.

She placed her hand in the crook of Harold's arm and received a gentle pat as the wedding march began, taking her closer to her heart's desire. Everything faded into the distance, except Drake and their love. The music ended and Harold kissed her cheek, stepping away. She slipped her hands into Drake's and knew there was nothing in the past to pull her back.

Their love would move them forward.

*

Selena left Drake talking with their guests and went to her room to change. The look in his eyes said he wouldn't wait much longer in keeping his hands off of her. Drake hadn't disclosed their honeymoon site, wanting it to be his secret. She was looking forward to finding out.

She spied the envelope where Tom had left it, thinking it was probably from Martha and Larry, whom she'd invited to the wedding.

Opening the seal, she tipped the envelope and a single picture of an infant boy and a several sheets of paper fell onto the table. It wasn't from Larry or Martha. She didn't know where it had come from.

She fumbled with a chair and sat down. The report, which read like the type of reports she'd filed when she was still with the Agency, confirmed that Theresa was dead—but stated that she'd left a son behind.

A son.

A member of the Donovan clan had married Theresa, gotten her pregnant—and now Selena had a nephew. The report further explained there was a contract on the infant but had hit dead ends after that. This wasn't the norm for hits as babies and women were not targets—just accidentals when their loved ones were taken out.

Her body shook from the emotional onslaught of sorrow and rage tearing at her heart as she forced herself to read the rest of the report.

And it was further discovered that Selena had an older sister—a sister by blood, not marriage, named Lilly.

Disbelief warred through her veins to the point of being unable to breathe.

She had been adopted by Theresa's parents. Nothing was

mentioned about Lilly's whereabouts. The investigator stated he was in the process of finding out Lilly's location and the name of their birth mother. It mentioned Drake's brother as being murdered by the Donovans. The more she read, the less she could feel, until numbness permeated every part of her mind and body. And then she read the part that changed her life.

Oh. My. God.

She was a Donovan.

The patriarch of the Donovan clan was Lilly's biological father. Worse, he was Selena's biological father.

She let the report drop from her nerveless fingers. She couldn't even begin to understand this.

But who had sent the report? Drake wouldn't have given this information to her in this manner.

Andrew Donovan was the father of her nephew. The man responsible for the death of her sister. The man she supposed was responsible for Lacey's abduction.

And the death of Drake's brother.

Leaving the agency, Selena had left too many ends unraveled. It was her mess and her mess only. She couldn't involve Drake and risk his life to a past she thought she'd left behind.

A scribbled note would not do justice to explanations on their wedding day. Her heart ached at the decision hanging between the past and a future with Drake. Her heart ached for what she was about to do, but she had no choice. Theresa's son was in danger. If she didn't go back to that world to get her nephew out, she wouldn't be able to live with herself. She prayed Drake would someday understand.

She did the only thing she was good at … heading back to the past of betrayals and lies, leaving her own web of deceit at not revealing her past to Drake.

Chapter Ten

Ten hours later

What in the world had she gotten herself into now? Selena glanced in the rearview mirror.

He wasn't following her.

Yet.

One by one she picked the pins out of her hair, letting them fall at gravity's will. He would never want her back now. Yet a part of her knew he'd never let her go either.

Especially when she had withheld something he'd been waiting for a long time. Hadn't he told her from the beginning he would collect? If she had been smart enough, she would've run like hell.

The last pin tumbled in between the seats, and dark soft curls drifted to her shoulders. She massaged the areas where pins had held her hair captive for the past ten hours and sighed. She'd left a mission unfinished.

And now she needed back in.

"Damn it, Theresa!" Selena pushed the car to ninety.

Larry had better come through for her or she would definitely bring his wife into the picture. She had never blackmailed anyone, but this wasn't a time to be angelic.

Not with her nephew's life at stake.

*

"You wouldn't dare!" White bellowed at the top of his lungs.

With his white hair and red face, he reminded her more of the Mad Hatter than a man who had ten grandchildren and about to become great-grandpa soon.

"Larry, I need to connect. What's a little trade here and there?"

"A little? Are you out of your ever-lovin' fu—freaking mind," Larry started to swear then toned it down. "What's in it for me? You had to fight your way out of here. You left us with nothing. Do you know how close you were in getting the information needed to put the Donovan family away?" Larry paced the length of his office, his posture as rigid as the expression on his face.

"Remember your—"

Larry glared at her. "And don't even open your pretty little mouth about my blood pressure. That knockout smile of yours won't budge this old coot a second time around. Nor will your little piece of blackmail."

"I prefer to think of it as a bargaining chip. Wasn't that the first thing you had taught me?" Selena smiled, knowing the effect it would have on him.

"If I could only—Wait a minute. Aren't you supposed to be somewhere today? Like on your ..."

"It's finished."

"Did you ever tell him about your past?"

Selena glared back, forgetting she was supposed to draw him on her side. "No. All he knows is what he's seen."

"Which is nothing?"

She hated when Larry smiled at her like that. As if he knew her better than she knew herself. "What was there to tell? If I told him anything of my past, I wouldn't be standing here." It was a fact she'd known a long time ago she would have to face.

"How much do you know about his past?"

"What does this have to do with my request?"

"Just answer my question."

She unclenched her hand and faced him. "I know he has secrets. Who doesn't? He was into search and rescue."

"You're a cold one, Malone." Larry shook his head and tapped her heart gently with his index finger. "Still cold enough to handle the proposition I'm about to give you, though."

Selena drew straight and waited. If she interrupted him now, he might change his mind.

"If I provide a single lead, nothing more, it's in your court to work this. I don't know why you want this particular lead, nor do I want you to tell me. Something tells me that in this situation, ignorance is bliss." Larry walked to his desk, pulled a key from his pocket and unlocked the bottom file cabinet labeled "touch and die."

Larry always had a way of words.

Still silent, she watched as he pulled the drawer open and pulled out a single manila envelope. He held it for a moment. Watching. Looking for some answer to an unasked question. What he didn't know wouldn't hurt him.

"This lead comes with a warning. So listen carefully, Malone."

She held back a shiver. Whenever he called her Malone, it was his way of telling her it was serious and she'd better pay attention.

"When you do with whatever it is you're about to do with this lead," he waited until he held eye contact before continuing. "You're in until the end. Should you need to get out for any reason, no one will help you. No one knows of your entrance back into this organization. The only thing people will know is that you are connected with the family and will be seen as the enemy and will have no problems taking you out. Take special care. When this is over, the truth will come out to your fellow agents. Until then ..."

She grasped the envelope offered to her. "I understand."

He stared into her eyes. "Do you? I wonder ..."

"Do you know anything about an envelope I received at my wedding?"

"When did it arrive?"

"Right before I walked down the aisle," she said, watching his reaction.

"Damn," he muttered. Then he said, "You should've told him."

Selena stopped, but didn't turn around. "Tell him what? That I no longer exist? I think he's already gotten the picture on that one."

*

Two hours and two cups of Starbuck's mocha cappuccino later, she still hadn't opened the envelope Larry had given her. Thankfully the air conditioning was off. It was freezing. Selena rubbed her bare arms. Larry's last words still resonated within her. *You should've told him.*

Something didn't smell right.

She pulled out her cell phone and dialed Larry's number. She counted the rings. One ring ... two rings ...

"Come on, White, I know you're there. You're expecting this call."

"Yes?"

"Spill."

Silence. He was intentionally drawing out the tension until she was ready to go through the line and bring him back face to face.

"White ..." she warned.

"What do you want me to spill?"

"Buying time won't help your case. You want me to know something? Then tell me. Don't play with words. Where have you and Drake met?"

"I wish you had gone on your honeymoon," Larry said. "I better not find your body on some riverbank or stuffed in the trunk of an abandoned car."

"Well, the travel agency booked me on this trip instead."

"Never blink an eye do you?"

Selena wished she could go back ten years and do this all over again.

"Selena, are you there?"

"Thinking," she said, looking down at the whipped cream drizzling out of the lid.

A special man came along once in a lifetime. Drake wouldn't forgive what she'd done to him.

After a moment she said, "Just doing some preplanning before meeting up with the past. Is there anyone in that part of the organization that might recognize me?"

"No one within the family." He hesitated.

"Okay. And before you say it, I remember the rules loud and clear. Don't tell Drake you talked to me."

"How did you figure it out?"

"Woman's intuition, my dear White." Selena smiled into the phone, her fingers traced the edge of the envelope. A very thin envelope. If she didn't know Larry as well as she did, she'd think it was empty.

Chapter Eleven

Drake Malone adjusted the lens. He'd thought the Agency was the answer to his restlessness. Surprisingly, he hadn't had to blackmail Larry into lifting the enforced leave. In fact, it had been a little too easy.

Selena was still gone. The detectives he'd hired came up with dead ends as far as Selena's family and friends went. Selena wasn't the most trusting women. She had kept her past from many of the townspeople.

Eight weeks and two days. That was how long it had been since she'd abandoned him—no note, no word. Just gone.

Drake stood from the rooftop of a neighboring building. He focused the binoculars on the crowd entering and leaving the restaurant across the street. His partner, Barry Prawn, was beside him and he handed over the binoculars so he could take a look. Andrew Donovan's group had been seated. There was no sign of Andrew's father, Don. But that didn't mean Don was giving up any control.

"Word has it he wants more grandchildren so bad he's ready to use modern technology if his own kids don't move a little faster. It's been said he has two daughters somewhere and wants to bring them into the empire."

"He's not thinking straight," Barry said.

Drake shook his head. "Don has this philosophy of immortality. He believes family bloodlines need to stay pure and unbroken."

He saw Barry's preoccupation wasn't in the direction of the stakeout; the binoculars were trained on a female figure seated at the restaurant but not at Donovan's table.

"The girl can wait, Barry. Maybe you can get her name and number after we're finished."

"You sure you don't wanna see what she looks like?" Barry smirked.

Drake didn't like that smile. "Dammit," he said, his voice low. When

Barry wouldn't let up, he scanned the direction of Barry's binoculars.

Drake let out a low whistle and smiled his appreciation. Taking a closer look, his lips flattened into a hard line, jaw clenched. He took several pictures. "We've got work to do," he snapped.

Andrew Donovan, the youngest of Don's kids, was seated with several bodyguards at tables outside a quaint Italian restaurant. Andrew was known for dealing first, then eating, unlike his old man who ate first, then accepted or declined any offers. Old man Donovan liked seeing them squirm, waiting for the outcome.

A man in his sixties with salt-and pepper-hair and a body boasting more of a keg than a six pack under a purple silk shirt came onto the scene. He sauntered over to the hostess. In his right ear was one chunk of diamond.

Drake laughed. "I'd recognize that earring anywhere. I never thought Martha would allow it out of her sight. She's going to kill him."

Barry's attention was once again distracted by the girl in the courtyard across the cobbled drive. "She's a hot one — "

"Shut up."

Barry gave him a startled look. "I'm just commenting — "

Drake looked at his friend again to see if he was putting one on him, and decided he wasn't. "Take another look at her."

Barry did.

*

Selena had lucked out, tipping a young waiter to seat her in plain sight of Andrew Donovan and his party. She sat at the table and drummed her fingers on her book. It was hard to believe she and Andrew came from the same genes. As soon as Andrew concluded his business, she would approach him—and Eric, her young nephew, whom he had with him.

A man encased in deep plum shirt crossed the street. She smiled at the white pants. When the man turned to greet Andrew, she nearly choked, grabbing the spray of coffee in time before it connected with another customer. She couldn't believe Larry had it in him. Hadn't he promised Martha he wouldn't enter the game ever again?

Larry shook Andrew Donovan's hand. Andrew snuffed the cigar with gentle strokes and gestured to the chair in front of him. Larry sat down. A young waiter started towards the table. One of the bodyguards glared at him. The restaurant's owner saw the mistake at the same time and steered the young waiter from Andrew's view.

Andrew frowned.

Selena had seen Larry in action before, and she saw now the way his eyes took everything in, yet gave the impression he was focusing on Andrew. She couldn't hear what Larry was saying, but Andrew seemed to like it.

Andrew folded his hands together in prayer fashion, resting his elbows on the table, index fingers on his lips. After a few moments, he waved to one of his men, who in turn signaled to the owner. Dishes of pasta, garlic bread, and wine made it to various checker-clothed tables for Andrew and his men.

Selena thanked God she had missed her sister's wedding. If she hadn't, Andrew would have recognized her and would never have allowed her this close to Eric.

There had only been a street and time listed in White's envelope. This place. Which she'd spent weeks checking out, studying who accompanied Andrew and how the meetings went.

She scanned the area for the rest of Larry's team—she knew Larry wasn't alone. This had to be pretty big if he'd been willing to come out from behind the desk. How in the hell was she supposed to do this if Larry had the place staked out?

It was now or never, she decided.

Selena pushed her chair back. The iron wrought chair scraped against brick. She placed her napkin on the table. She gritted her teeth mentally and plastered an airhead smile for the men as she crossed the street.

Damn Larry.

Where would he put his men? The cobbled courtyard overflowing with soft music and tropical plants would be the best seat in the house. Two other cafés sat at the dead-end street and one on the other corner. It was a silent agreement no one reported what took place within their establishments.

Several suited men at the outside bar laughed with a waiter whose white apron was wrapped around his waist and who balanced a tray with one hand. The waiter patted one of them on the back.

The men were regulars.

Book and purse in hand, she headed towards the courtyard where Andrew sat. Where the hell were Larry's men?

A baby squealed. She turned without even thinking and stared in Andrew's direction, spotting her nephew, Eric. Even from here, she could see his huge dimpled smile resembled Theresa's. Had he inherited her birthmark?

A broad-shouldered man, bulging with muscles and a gun under his coat, placed the six-month-old Eric in his stroller. The man turned to chat with a girl selling flowers from a basket on her arm.

Selena would recognize that pitted face anywhere even if the Agency's reports hadn't described him. They called him Poxy due to the scars of chicken pox from his childhood. Though no one said it to his face.

It would be so easy to take Eric when he wasn't looking. Sometimes having a single man take care of a baby was a bad idea; his other needs became more important when a pretty girl was around. She wished it would be that simple to snatch and run, but with a family like the Donovans, there was a lot of gun-power to follow.

Selena casually turned toward the waiter who had appeared from a darkened alcove.

"May I help you?" he offered.

She smiled and looked over the top of her sunglasses. "Yes.

Thank you. A table for one outside if they're not reserved."

"For a pretty young lady like you … anything is possible." His eyes strayed to her tanned shoulders as if he wanted to touch. Instead he led her to a sunny spot three tables away from where Poxy sat with Eric, which was far enough from Larry's meeting with her brother for her to feel comfortable sitting there.

The waiter pulled out a chair. She accepted. Larry seemed to notice how close the waiter had placed her and frowned. Andrew watched her and said something to Larry. Larry shook his head and Andrew returned to business at hand.

The waiter offered to bring her something to drink.

"I would love an iced tea with a lime on the side." She laid her book on the table, a hollow prop with her gun tucked inside. Selena loved being outdoors and if this had been an ordinary day, she would've been enjoying the surroundings and atmosphere. Instead she felt tense and wary.

Two businessmen across the cobbled street kept staring at her. She raised her brow at the one scowling and ignored him. She drummed her fingers on the book. *Come on, Larry where are your men?* She had already discounted the businessmen. A few ladies sat next to the wall of tropical plants, sipping margaritas.

Larry stood up.

Andrew gestured for him to remain.

Larry wiped his mouth, folded his napkin slowly as he shook his head and laid it on the table.

She looked back at the two businessmen sitting a little too close to be "only friends." Guys usually wanted a little more space to call their own. She ran her eyes up the backside of the older one, who was sporting a hearing aid. His partner seemed a little stiff, as if they'd recently had a spat. The older one grinned as he patted his companion's shoulder.

Selena laughed.

A shot rang out, shattering a carafe at the table next to her. Selena threw herself down to the ground, scanning her environment. Where had the shot come from? Andrew's bodyguards were on their feet, moving and shouting. Had one of Andrew's many enemies taken a potshot at him?

She shifted, seeing the two businessmen from across the street charging toward the chaos. Toward the chaos—that meant they were Larry's men. She dismissed them, and saw that Eric's stroller was exposed. She leaped toward it but one of Larry's men took her down, his body becoming a hard shield.

"Stay down," he warned in her ear.

She tried to push him off, but he refused to move. And that was when she knew—Selena's body hummed with need. His head moved downward, capturing her lips. She tasted desire, yearning, and unanswered questions.

The kiss was too familiar, haunting her body in a way she had wanted to forget because no one could take the place of her husband. The way he caressed her cheek with his thumb after kissing her possessively.

Apparently, Larry had more to answer for than she thought.

"Hey, Drake, catch up with her later," a young man's voice interrupted them.

"We will finish this later," Drake promised, following his partner.

There was no time for regrets or hunger. Eric had been placed in danger and she hadn't prevented it. She looked over at the restaurant where her nephew had sat. She could have grabbed Eric and run, but there were too many guns. Too many bullets. And too many of Andrew's henchmen to run from. By now, Andrew and his men had vanished, leaving overturned tables and chairs.

A crunch under her foot made her stop in her tracks. She crouched down and gingerly picked up the cracked rattle. Another few feet away lay Eric's dinosaur. She picked it up and caressed the red-stained belly. She surveyed the food-splattered courtyard.

Sighing, she shook the sauce from the dinosaur.

It didn't help not knowing if Eric was alive or dead.

She had failed her main objective.

To protect Eric.

In the end, today would only serve to deepen Andrew's protection over his son. She had lost an opportunity to grab him. There was no way she'd get another chance like this.

God help the man who tried to fulfill the contract against her nephew's life.

And God help the man who put him on that list to begin with.

She dug a plastic bag out of the car and placed Eric's dinosaur in it.

Whoever thought he could end Eric's life had just screwed with his own life expectancy.

Chapter Twelve

Larry wasn't answering his phone. She pressed redial. *Answer the phone, Larry.* Two more rings. Larry's voice mail answered. "I don't care who you are, thirty seconds is all you have." Beep.

"Larry, honey ... My ride left without me." She could feel the adrenaline flowing wild. Her heart raced with a burning need to go for the kill. She set the phone on the seat and leaned back, frustrated at the outcome and worried Andrew would think she was involved in the set-up to take him out.

Now was not the time for this, she reprimanded herself. She needed a clear head and a new plan. Coffee was the next best thing to walking in doing this.

Selena knew there was a coffee house down the street and headed that way. She had taken time to scout the area, using the coffee house as a source of establishing herself within the small neighborhood. A bell chimed as she entered. As warm as it was outside she needed something frozen, loaded with whipped cream, fudge sauce, and caffeine. Without looking at the menu, she chose the mocha-coconut frappucino.

She pulled a few ones from the pockets of her low-riding jeans.

"Bad day?" Claire, the manager, asked.

"It'll get better," Selena answered, unaware of the heat in her voice. She handed the money to the girl.

A male hand pushed her money back her way. "It's mine."

"No, thank you. I can pay my own way," she said without looking at the owner of the well-manicured hand.

"Are you sure you want to refuse this offer?"

The craggy voice forced her to look into the man's eyes.

"Is this man bothering you?" asked Claire.

She couldn't tear her eyes away from the pitted face.

The wrinkles gave away his age, but what gave it away even more were the eyes. A Donovan through and through. His nickname—Pitter Patter Man—didn't begin to capture his menace.

She forced herself to continue meeting his gaze, despite the outstretched frozen drink.

Pitter Patter Man took the drink and placed it in her hand.

"Take the man's money. It's his turn to pay anyways," Selena said without taking her eyes from him.

Claire shook her head. The other customers did a one-hundred-eighty degree turn-around when they saw this man. Selena didn't blame them. When Claire tried to give him his change, he shook his head without looking in her direction, his eyes on Selena.

Claire's expression suggested she didn't like this one bit. Several babies cried out.

Pitter Patter Man gave each baby several seconds of his focus. The babies stopped crying instantly, returning the stare. Mothers turned their babies from his attention.

He smiled at the protective mothers.

Customers made way for Pitter Patter as he headed out the door. He gestured with a quick nod at the car waiting outside. Selena knew it was meant for her. How the Donovan family knew she was here was beyond her comprehension. But then … there were some people willing to sell anything and everyone for money or favors.

Unconsciously she set the drink next to the lids and straws and followed him out. Pitter Pan Man disappeared. In his place, a driver appeared and opened a door, waiting for her to slide inside of the extended limo.

She hesitated.

A baby laughed.

Was it Eric? This time she didn't think twice and stepped inside.

"Ms. Malone. I see you survived in one piece," Andrew said, nodding to his driver.

The driver closed the door.

She watched Eric from the corner of her eye. Even if she was carrying, she would never shoot with Eric in close proximity. He was so much like her sister. The dimples. The blonde hair.

"Yes, I survived." Why bother acting dumb. "As you did."

"Well, I've been known to have the luck of the Irish." Andrew laughed.

Selena watched Eric's reaction. He didn't move. Interesting.

"My son, Eric. My only son."

"He looks like his daddy." Andrew's face contorted with a sliver of momentary anger.

"What did you wish to talk to me about?" she asked.

"I saw you reaching for my son."

"I meant no harm."

"But you tried to grab him. I saw it with my own eyes."

Her heart raced. "May I explain?"

"No need."

The limo began to slow down.

"It's a simple explanation — "

Andrew stroked Eric's head until Eric lay against him, closing his eyes. "I don't doubt it. But once I see it, no explanations are necessary." Andrew pushed a button.

"Sir?" the driver voice asked over the intercom. The car came to a complete stop.

"Ms. Malone will no longer be riding with us."

The door beside her opened and the driver waited for her to get out.

Keeping herself in check without allowing fear for her nephew's safety to overwhelm her, she nodded towards Andrew, refusing to look at Eric. The pain was too great to swallow.

"You are a strong woman, Ms. Malone. My wife would've liked to have called you a friend."

"I would've loved to have met your wife, Mr. Donovan." And she meant it.

She accepted the driver's help out. Another car had pulled up behind them, waiting to take her away. Her weapon was tucked under the seat of her car and even if she had her cell phone on her, any help would be too late in coming. A white-haired man stepped partway out of the car, one foot resting inside the car, his arm draped over the top of the door.

Lifting her chin up in defiance, she walked his way and got in the car.

The driver didn't have that look of pleasure some guys have when they were about to kill. He was very relaxed, smiling as he shut the door behind her.

Andrew, on the other hand, had been extremely tense. Who wouldn't be after having his life threatened? She could see how her sister had fallen for Andrew. Out of all the Donovan males, he was very handsome. Sort of a pretty boy look with his dark hair. He had a slight gut on him but considering how much he enjoyed food that was to be expected. Despite the tightness about him, he was very polite.

"Where are we going?" she asked.

"Which way to your place?"

She did a double take. "My place?"

"You'll need your things."

Now she was confused. "Why?"

He snorted. "Females are a little dense these days. Don't understand what Mr. Donovan sees in you. His wife was extremely intelligent, but he knows his own mind. Never knew when he didn't."

She gave him directions. "What do they call you?"

"Not much for pleasantries."

She laughed. "I don't think you'd come if I whistled to the theme of *The Sopranos*."

He guffawed. "No, but it's good entertainment." He pulled in front of her temporary rental. "You have thirty minutes to gather what you'll need. What you don't get, I'm sure it can be replaced."

"Thirty minutes?" She sounded like a parrot.

"Mr. Donovan's orders. If you're not done in thirty minutes, you come as you are. It's Tony."

Inwardly, she sighed. She'd been out of the loop too long. This conversation was not making any sense.

*

Thirty minutes and one suitcase later, they were on their way. Luckily Tony hadn't seen the empty apartment or the packed suitcase already sitting in the foyer. She had passed time going to the bathroom and trying Larry's number once again. No luck.

Once Selena was back in the car, she found a piece of bubblegum and popped it in her mouth. She blew bubbles, smacked her lips with each chew, and asked a gazillion questions guaranteed to blow any man's mind. Each time she whooshed her gum back inside her mouth and mashed it, Tony cringed. If she had to be off guard, then they might as well do it together.

The ride was scenic and long compared to her city driving of ten minutes here and ten minutes there. Tony finally pulled up to a gated house. A few seconds later the gate slid open.

A large white veranda followed the full length of the house and around the corner on the first and second levels. An ornate water fountain stood in the center of the circular drive. She counted at least ten armed men patrolling the area.

Tony parked in the circular drive and indicated that she could get out. The sweet fragrance of flowers greeted her as she did so.

Andrew came out of the front door to greet her. "Good evening, Ms. Malone. I see Tony brought you in one piece."

Selena smiled back, offering her hand in acknowledgement. "Tony was a superb host, Mr. Donovan. I'm not sure I was the perfect guest."

"Call me Andrew."

She followed him through the foyer into a small library off to the side. "Why have you brought me here, Mr.—Andrew? I'm not sure what you're expecting of me."

"To be blunt, you saved my life and my son's. I want to repay you."

"I didn't do anything."

"You put yourself between one of the assailants and my son," Andrew said.

"I don't need anything for doing that."

He looked down at the shoes, worn jeans, and frayed shirt she had changed into for comfort. His smile wasn't unkind. "You need a job and I need someone for my son. Since his mother had passed away, the boy needs female company. Later in life? That's a different story. But for now, he needs a mother figure."

"I could never replace your wife." And she couldn't. No one could replace her sister—or a mother's love.

"Why don't you try the job out? If you don't think it's for you, well ..."

Who was he kidding? This family had never allowed anyone to quit.

"You've got yourself a deal."

"Mary will show you to your room. If you need anything else just ask her and she'll see that you get it. My drivers will take you wherever you need to go. Give me the name of your banking institution and I'll have your account credited with your weekly salary."

An elderly woman entered the room. A silver bun adorned the back of her head, her dress matronly. "You wanted me?"

"See to it Ms. Malone has everything she needs."

Selena reached out to shake hands. "Nice to meet you, Mary. Please call me Selena."

Mary gave her the once over, sniffed, and walked out.

"Mary is a woman of few words. She'll get used to you. It just takes her time in getting to know newcomers," Andrew remarked.

She turned to follow Mary.

"Selena ..."

She stopped in the archway.

"I treat my loyal employees well. I treat my family even better."
Selena caught up with Mary at the head of the stairs. As Mary
opened the door to Selena's bedroom, a warm breeze swept past
them. Mary headed towards the open windows.

"Please don't close them." Mary continued closing them.
Selena walked over and stood next to her. Mary faced her. "I love
fresh air. Please don't shut the windows." Mary shrugged as if to
say her loss.

"Thank you, Mary." No answer.

Selena sat down on the floral cushion by the bay window and
sighed. Usually housekeepers were a rich source of information.
Not this one. She had to hand it to Mary, the room she'd been
given was beautiful.

The four-poster bed ensemble and the curtains matched the
window seat. There was a small adjoining sun room with ferns
and furniture for lounging with French doors opening onto the
balcony. With the exception of the tapestry hanging at the head of
the bed, the walls were bare. Upon closer inspection, she noticed
the faint lines where frames had once hung.

"Used to be Miss Theresa's room."

Then Mary was gone.

It would be difficult to pin her sister's death on the Donovans
since Theresa couldn't speak for herself. Had Theresa continued
her youthful journalizing? If so, perhaps there would be some
useful evidence. When Theresa was in high school, her favorite
hiding place was under the bed, tucked along the slats. If this had
been Theresa's room, then there was only one way to find out.

Lying on her back, Selena used her hands and feet to push
herself partway under the bed. She felt between the mattress and
each of the slats, starting with the middle one. "Ah ha. Here it is.
Theresa, you are a saint," Selena whispered, pulling the leather-
bound journal out.

Something brushed against her face. She stifled a scream

and moved quickly. The thought of Theresa keeping a journal had pushed her fear of spiders and tight spaces out of her mind. She walked to the door, opened it a few inches, and scouted the hallway. Seeing no one around, she held the knob and closed it without making a sound. She was sure her sister had written everything down, giving Andrew a free ticket into prison.

The small grandfather clock on the nightstand read ten till six. She glanced back at the book in her hands. Her fingers itched to turn the pages. She couldn't take the chance until everyone had fallen asleep. Theresa may have had a hard time admitting she'd made a mistake marrying Andrew, but her journal held the truth and would provide the final justice.

She tucked the book back under the bed. Dinner would be announced soon, summoning her downstairs. She wasn't prepared for being included with the family meals and hadn't packed suitable clothes. She hefted the suitcase on the bed. Placing what she needed to in the drawers, she opened the closet door and walked in. There wasn't one hanger free for her clothing. Andrew had stocked it well, anticipating someone to be wearing them. She found a tag and whistled at the price. Apparently, someone had taste.

"Do you like them?" Andrew asked.

Damn. She would have to remember how quiet he could be.

He joined her inside the closet.

She pulled a cream colored dress off the rack and dipped inside the silk for the label. It was definitely her size. "You work fast."

"I have my ways." He flipped through the rack, found what he'd been searching for, pulled it out and held the sable-colored dress up to her. "Wear this." Bending down, he found suede heels to match it. He brushed the suede with his thumb and then stroked his thumb across her cheek. "Just as I'd thought."

When Andrew left, she rubbed his touch away from her skin. He had excellent taste in clothes, but he didn't have one ounce of heart in that body. He'd clearly signaled his intentions. He wanted her for more than a nanny.

By the time she'd dressed and gone down to the dining room, everyone was seated for dinner with the exception of Andrew, who waited behind a chair.

Old man Don turned at the sound of her entrance. His older son, Terrance, didn't spare more than a single glance. Several of the Donovans' henchmen were seated with them.

Andrew's eyes trailed down the length of her body, hesitating a little longer on the curves emphasized by the soft, hugging material. He pulled her chair out, taking time to view her backside.

She saw no other available seating and accepted gracefully.

None of these men were like the man she'd left behind. She hoped Drake would forgive her for running out on him. Judging from the expression in his eyes at the stakeout, he hadn't looked happy. Of course, she couldn't blame him. He had more than just one beef with her.

Especially since she had made him wait until after they were married.

Andrew fingered her hair before taking his seat.

"So when are my children going to produce more babies?" Don asked, breaking into her private thoughts and the conversations around the table. "My youngest is the only one with enough balls to keep practicing until his wife died. And she produced a boy." Everyone grew extremely quiet at the edge in Don's voice.

Terrance folded his hands and rested them on the edge of the table; his beer-keg belly made sitting close to the table difficult. His face grew redder by the second. "Don't push."

"Have you born any grandbabies for me to hold?"

"Listen ol—" Terrance stopped. His eyes followed the slow movement of Don's fingers to the side of the plate. "With all due respect, Don," he said. "I haven't met a woman who would meet with your approval."

"That's rich. You've found plenty to screw. And you haven't found one good enough to marry?"

Andrew placed his fork on the plate.

Both Terrance and Old Don immediately noticed the clench and release of Andrew's jaw.

Terrance resumed eating.

Old Don moved his fingers to his napkin, with reluctance.

In just that tiny little action made more of a statement than the scene that had just taken place. Andrew held more power than Terrance. Maybe Eric's ability to carry on the family name had something to do with it.

"The room is beautiful, Mr. Donovan. I understand it used to be Mrs. Donovan's room. I feel very privileged. Thank you."

Andrew frowned, but quickly hid it behind his glass of red wine. He polished off the last of it and replenished the glass before answering, "It's Andrew. You are free to change anything you want."

"I wouldn't touch a thing in it," Selena said as she dabbed the side of her mouth with her napkin. "By the way, Andrew, what was the attached room used for?"

Andrew's movements stilled and his mouth tightened at the corners briefly before he rested his wrist on the edge of the table.

She waited with the others, who had also stopped whatever they were doing for a second time to hear his answer. Several times his facial expression changed, each fleeting, but noticeable to someone in her field.

"It was the baby's room. When Theresa died, Mary took over the care of little Eric's needs and moved him into her room."

Selena wanted to shout, *When Theresa was murdered!* All faces were devoid of emotion. Great poker faces. Not one ounce of humanity in this den of murderers, slavers, and drug runners.

"Theresa had an extra room she'd used for sewing and thought it would be easier if we converted it for Eric. Mary didn't want to use it after Theresa died."

He was lying.

Each word was too controlled. Too much effort in keeping the emotions in check.

"I want to start earning my keep, Andrew. It would be easier for me to do that if he were brought back to the nursery," she offered.

Andrew filled his glass with more wine. "You'll have to take that up with Mary. She protects Eric as a tiger protects her young," he said, dryly. He raised his glass towards the kitchen door and nodded.

Selena followed the direction of his salute.

Mary stood in doorway, glaring at Andrew, her lips pursed tight. She gave quick jerk of her head before turning back into the kitchen. The door slammed shut behind her.

Andrew laughed. "See what I mean? Our Mary can be very formidable when she wants to be. Even Father won't go against Mary. Isn't that right?"

Old Don ignored the baited question.

*

When Selena returned to her room, she knew someone had searched it. Most people wouldn't have noticed the slight opening of the top drawer or the light on in the closet. They didn't suspect she would notice, taking her for a fluff brain. She didn't bother checking her personal items since nothing would've been taken. It wasn't personal. Searching their employees was only business for the Donovans.

If they found her sister's journal, Selena was dead. She was impatient to see if it was still in place.

"I see you found your way back."

Andrew stood two feet away.

She laughed. "I'm one of those people who look for landmarks on the first time through and then try it on their own."

Andrew's lips curled in distaste. "I never did like this room or the colors. Theresa fell in love with it, too. My mother's room," he explained. "It hasn't been changed since her death. Theresa wanted to remember my mother. Said she felt a connection with her. Don't know why though. They'd never met."

He looked over at the bay window. A shudder passed through him. "I'll let Mary know you'll be in charge of Eric. It may take a few days, but ..." He hesitated and shrugged as if she knew what he meant. "Go ahead and tour the house. I'd take you, but I'm wrapped up in meetings for the rest of the week. In case you get cabin fever and want to walk, let one of the men know. My father is a wealthy man and so am I, in my own right, so we need to practice extreme caution. My men will follow you. Discreetly, of course."

Andrew paused at the door. "I like you, Selena. There's a familiarity between us I can't explain. You're not as ditzy as you let on." She didn't allow her surprise to show. "I want you to be my wife. I want you in my bed within three months. That's all the time I'll allow you to get used to the idea. I won't accept less than marriage. Nor will I accept a refusal."

Selena's mouth dropped open.

He smiled. Then he was gone.

She smothered the laughter bubbling inside. The man she'd left behind was a man of few words, preferring action over words. No matter how hard he had tried to get her into bed, she had refused. Too many emotional strings to deal with. Although she'd had a few relationships, she preferred keeping men at a distance.

Easier. Less heartache.

She sighed and quickly changed into sweats and T-shirt. She peeked outside her door. The household noise had dwindled to a few voices here and there. The hall was empty.

Quickly closing the door, she snatched the book from its hiding spot and nestled into the huge down-filled pillows on the bed. She caressed the embossed lettering. Tears pooled in her eyes. The only things she had left of Theresa were memories and Eric.

"Theresa, I miss you so much. Please don't worry, Eric will be safe. I swear this on my own life," she whispered. The tears slid down her face before she could wipe them away.

It was hard opening the pages to her sister's private world ...

Chapter Thirteen

Dear Journal,

I can't believe Selena isn't coming to my wedding. I wanted her to meet Andrew and I understand her flight was delayed. I could hear the tears in her voice when she told me she wouldn't make it. At the same time I was so disappointed I couldn't stop yelling at her. Wedding jitters, I suppose.

The writing trailed off as if Theresa's hand had slipped and there were two small discolorations. Selena wished she could've read this where she could grieve in private, but grieving would have to wait.

Andrew just left. He heard me crying. I knew I wouldn't be able to not cry. He came in and held me. That's one of the reasons I fell for him even though he gets so moody and unpredictable around his father. He wants to start a family right away. He says the more boys we have, the happier his father will be. I'd rather take this time to be alone with him first.

Dear Journal,

I can't believe it! Our honeymoon was out of this world. Andrew had a few anxieties, but that's something we can overcome together. And we did during the trip. He rented horses and we rode along the family's private beach. I was surprised he even went out on the boogey boards and tried to ride the waves. And now, the moment we come home, Andrew is distant and moody. He's working all the time, rarely spending any time with me. I guess the honeymoon is over. I know he's been upset over those nights making love, but I thought we'd gotten through all of that. I tried to talk to him and I know it wasn't the best way to handle it, but I suggested counseling. He blew his top and started ranting and raving. God forbid a Donovan ever see a shrink. I've never seen him lose his cool before and it scared me. Two years without a cigarette and here I am lighting up. Gotta go, journal. Someone's knocking on my door.

Selena closed the book and placed it on her chest. What anxieties did Andrew experience on his honeymoon? Who had placed the hit on Eric?

Two short knocks came into the night's silence.

Selena's eyes flew open. She hadn't realized her eyes had been shut until now.

"Yes?"

The doorknob turned but the door didn't open.

"Is it okay if I enter?" Andrew asked through the door, his voice low.

She yanked the covers over her body, ran her fingertips through her hair several times. "Yes," Selena said.

She noticed the light and doused it. The book. The last thing she remembered was setting it aside as she snuggled under the covers. She scanned the bed and then leaned over to the one side and looked.

The door opened.

She flopped against the pillows. Wherever it was, it'd better stay hidden until he was gone.

Andrew slipped through the partially opened door. He wore black lounging bottoms and nothing else but the hair on his chest. He was relaxed and smiling. She could see why Theresa had been attracted to this man.

Almost.

"I see you're settled in for the night. I can come back another time perhaps," he said, his eyes black with need and anger at not being received with more eagerness.

"Now is fine. I hadn't fallen asleep, just drowsy. Sometimes it takes me awhile to fall asleep." At least ever since she'd left Drake to handle everything, including the night that was supposed to follow their wedding.

Andrew had stopped halfway between the door and her bed. "I don't think my meaning was clear at dinner."

"I understood. I'll give Mary time to adjust to a new nanny. I'd feel the same way if I were in her shoes."

His eyes narrowed. "Not that. Do you realize why you were hired?"

"Because your son needed a nanny?"

"Mary could, and would, prefer to do the care herself. There's another reason why you are caring for my son." He smiled. "The bed is too big for one person. I don't know why my mother chose it, but it looks good under you."

She smiled back. "I'm sure I'll get used to it."

He advanced a few more steps. Selena had made her meaning loud and clear. "I won't wait forever for you to invite me in."

"I sleep alone."

He sighed. Hand on one of the posts, he leaned closer. "I thought you were the intelligent one. The only reason I'm putting little Eric in your care is so you can get used to the idea of having a child."

Keep your head on, Selena, she warned herself, stilling her urge to kick him where it would hurt. Her hand strayed to the edges of blanket. She stopped herself from sighing with relief as her hand grazed the journal beneath it.

"I don't want to take a job if I'm not needed," she said, pushing herself into a sitting position.

"I had two business appointments scheduled earlier today before those men shot at my family. The first one was for my father, although I didn't get to enjoy my dinner. The second meeting was for me. I had someone searching for … shall we say … candidates," he finished with a wave of the hand.

It dawned on her. He hadn't been putting her on earlier. He'd really meant marriage.

She couldn't help it; she laughed. Andrew was her brother. "You thought I was one of those candidates. I wish I could say I was the right partner for you, but I haven't felt the want or the need for a man in my life." Besides, Drake had spoiled her for any other man.

Andrew waited for her to finish and she knew from the way he checked her out, he was satisfied.

He touched her thigh. His eyes were glazed with a sickness she'd never noticed before.

Instinctively, she moved her leg. Only one person had the right to touch her and he wasn't here. She sucked her breath in at the thought of Drake's touch.

Andrew sat on the bed, patting her leg. He'd misinterpreted her reaction. She couldn't stop from pulling away, but he continued anyways. "It's okay. You need time. Although you don't have unlimited time, you do have some time while I finish tying up the loose end of a personal matter."

He stood up and left as silently as he'd entered.

She shivered. Not from the sexual innuendos but from the unwelcome experience of having another man touching her. She willed herself to rise up from the bed and lock the door. She didn't want to fight off any more unwanted advances. Not taking any chances, she grabbed the book and placed it in its original hiding place and hopped back into bed, this time throwing her bottoms on the floor, keeping her boy shorts on. She preferred sleeping in the nude, but it was better to be prepared than to wake up being straddled by a sex-craved maniac who needed to buy a wife instead of finding one the natural way.

His words, "I thought you were the intelligent one," were the last thing on her mind before she fell fast asleep.

*

The dream man played with her tonight.

There wasn't a thing she could do to stop him.

She hated her lack of control. It had taken her all she had not to give into her own desires and run back to the past. What had started out as wondering if Drake was relationship material had changed to seeing how long he could maintain his self-control until their wedding night. She had no problems adding fuel to his fire.

His eyes were black with desire in the moonlit room, promising her sweet release. His laugh was rough, though not unpleasant.

She shivered and couldn't stop the hiss of desire seeping into the air.

He pulled off his black boots without taking his eyes from her. He undid the button on his black jeans.

She couldn't move.

He braced his hands on the bedposts and leaned forward. His eyes darkened with need.

Her body betrayed her. And it showed as he reached for her, spreading her legs.

His smile was all revenge.

He was about to collect on her broken promise.

This dream man had the power to freeze every thought and movement except the hidden desires heating up between them.

His eyes approved the body-hugging boy shorts.

"No man will have you but me," he said. "Did you think I wouldn't find you?"

His eyes dared her to deny him again. Dared her to deny the desire she felt. He smiled as if he knew she would willingly grant him access for one stroke of his touch.

He tugged the shorts off and tossed them away.

Her hips lifted for his touch, aching for release. He held them in place as he tasted the sweet betrayal. His tongue dipped inside the core center of her heat and devoured every drop. Letting her hips fall gently, he covered her mouth with his hand as his tongue stroked a nipple. She screamed into his hand. Her body reacted instantly to the heat he packed, grinding in short upward motions, seeking more. The dream man captured her hands and held them fast above her head before she managed to gain control. He laughed at her frustration and kissed her neck.

Her breath hitched with each kiss.

"Shh," he said quietly. He began whispering things, making her wish this was all real so she could rid herself of the building frustration inside before she exploded.

She bit his hand.

He laughed, but kept it in place as he reached lower, stroking. She held her breath. He lifted a finger to his mouth and tasted. She closed her eyes, praying he would finish what he had started. When he plunged his fingers back inside, pushing deeper, again and again, she knew she would be unable to deny him. He stopped.

She bucked harder, frantically trying to free her hands so she could either push him away or flip him on his back and take over.

It was useless. She wouldn't be free unless he let go on his own.

"How does it feel to want something so bad you can taste it? To lose control of your emotions? When I get the chance, I will take you to a place you wish you'd stayed. I don't know what the hell is going on, Selena," he whispered, looking into her eyes.

She tried to move away only to find herself locked in place.

The dream had become a reality.

He was not her dream man but the man she'd left with questions and needs unanswered.

He was as real as her desire.

She bucked harder, trying push him away.

"Honey, you know the saying about a woman scorned? Well, let me tell you ...When you give a man promises of ecstasy and fulfillment for waiting and then leave him high and dry ... a woman scorned doesn't hold a candle to what I want to do to you at this moment. But it can wait until there's no risk of being interrupted or you running away."

Suddenly she was free of him. The heat vanished instantly, her body limp and bereft.

He had the skills and speed of a cat. He was dressed and standing next to the open French doors in no time flat.

"How did you get in without tripping the alarms?" she managed to get out.

"You figure it out. But I think you have bigger problems, because I won't be responsible for what I do to your admirer should he touch you again." With one foot on the balcony, "I don't know what game you're playing or whose game you're willing to play ... Remember, you are mine. Until death do us part, Selena."

Frustrated as hell, and knowing anything she threw his way would only bring Andrew running, she resisted the urge. Not to mention Eric's life depended on her maintaining her control.

She hated surprises. And hated the fact he had been able to get inside her room with her unaware. "Drake," she whispered into the night air, taking both handles in her hands. "You will not see me lose control again." And locked the doors.

*

Drake patted his heart, reminding himself of what she was to him.

Part of him had no doubt after seeing her up close that she didn't belong here, but he couldn't, for the life of him, understand what the hell it was that brought her to a house which dealt in slavery. Selena didn't have the exotic beauty Andrew sold, but there was a beauty no woman could touch when she was vibrant and full of attitude. It had sucked him dry waiting and wondering how she would react when they finally made love.

Now he knew.

Larry hadn't blinked an eye at the stakeout when he passed Selena. He had a lot to answer for and when Drake got his hands on him, Larry would be buying him lobster and crab legs for as long as he lived.

Drake watched as Selena's curvy silhouette climbed into bed. It would be a while before she fell asleep. In the morning he would care if she had enough sleep to keep her wits about her, but for now, he was content knowing she was lying in bed, seething with the same wants and needs he'd had for the past nine weeks.

In no way would he call them even.

He signaled and waited. The go-ahead came. He scaled down the wall a few feet before he heard the cry. Inwardly, he groaned and signaled his intent to check it out. Using night vision goggles, he scoped Selena's room. There were traces of tears on her face.

The crying grew louder.

Within seconds he landed back on the balcony. He signaled and turned to listen for the sound again. The wait wasn't long.

Another cry came from the other side of the door. The crying softer, almost crooning. A rocker sat in the corner. The powder blue-and-white checkered cushion was empty.

He shook his head. Too little sleep could be dangerous for someone in his position.

Chapter Fourteen

Larry was at his computer.

The box read, "u & i need 2 talk"

"c u soon"

Larry typed in, "Now is not the time. I am not even in the office." Larry hated instant messenger even more than e-mails. He'd never gotten the hang of condensing words or using letters and numbers to do the trick.

Another message appeared. "liar. ur car is here" Then: "u better b ready 2 spill"

That was when Larry knew who he was talking to.

Drake.

And if he knew anything about Drake, Drake was already here. Probably standing outside his door with his smart phone. His wife had the same one and it even took pictures. He swiveled towards the window and craned his neck to look in the parking lot below. Even five stories high, Drake's vehicle would be easy to spot.

"Looking for my wheels?"

Larry swore and turned back towards his door.

Drake leaned against the frame.

"Wheels my ass. That's a tank sitting out there. Whatever you're getting paid is too much. I can't even afford to buy one of those."

"You're full of it, Larry. And you know I'm worth every penny."

"What's going on with Selena?"

"You won't like it."

"Screw liking it," Drake said, eyes narrowed. "The background on Selena."

"Technically, you're not even supposed to be on this case. I've broken enough rules this month." Seeing the stubborn set of

Drake's jaw changed his mind. "Aw hell, if I'm going out, I might as well go out with a bang. You can ask three questions. That's it."

"What is Selena's real name?"

That was easy. "Selena Malone."

"Our side or theirs?"

Larry couldn't tell him the truth. Her background was taboo. She was his only lead into the family. The Donovans hadn't placed the connection between Theresa and Selena. What no one knew was the Agency had intended to convince her to finish the job. Or blackmail her back. Larry was glad she had blackmailed him into giving her information on Andrew's habits. It made the taste in his mouth less bitter.

He knew if Selena ever found out, or Drake, he was a dead man.

"Hers," Larry said.

Drake's eyes narrowed to mere slits, his mouth flattened.

"What the hell is she up to?"

"I don't know. If you want to know ask her," Larry answered with a smile, glad to have gotten out of firing range.

Drake smiled back. "I will."

A man shoved past Drake.

Drake stopped cold. "Got a burr about something, Fry?"

Jeremy Fry, right-hand man to Larry's boss, shot back, "Only if you screw up again, Carpoli. I'll have you knee-deep in red tape if you don't take the Donovans down this time. Find the link."

Drake took a step forward and watched with a smile as Jeremy started to back up. In this business if you backed down from another man, your balls were questioned.

Jeremy leaned against White's desk.

"So what do you think about the new addition to the Donovan family?" He folded his arms over his chest.

Jeremy's cell phone rang. As he checked the caller, Drake caught sight of a small tattoo snaking out from Fry's T-shirt to the back of his neck. It hadn't been there five months ago when Jeremy had been transferred to this unit.

"Do you mean the leak? He's a dead man." To Larry, "Keep baby face in his own crib or he's going to be growing up real quick."

Both watched Drake leave the room and faced the window at the same time to view his departure. The Hummer spoke volumes about the man driving: *If you want me, here I am.*

After thirty minutes of dealing with one huge pain in the ass named Jeremy, Larry drifted back to an earlier conversation. He had no doubts Drake would find out Larry's part in the monkey wrench that had torn his wedding night to shreds. He just didn't want to be around when Drake did.

He had another option. Martha had been after him to take a vacation. He picked up the phone. "Dorothea," he told his assistant, "Get your travel agency on the line."

*

It took all his willpower to snap out of it. Drake kicked off his shoes and was greeted by Lady. He ruffled the top of her head. Lady wagged her tail. She'd wandered in his yard a few weeks ago, matted fur and ribs sticking out. He'd been asleep in his hammock, dreaming about another lady when he found himself face down in the grass. A cold nose nudged his ear. The breed was hard to see under the mud-coat, but the drool wasn't.

The dog had eyed his forgotten sandwich in the dust. In a matter of seconds, the front of his coat, and the ground, had become wet. Long strands of saliva had hung from each side of the dog's mouth.

He took the kerchief around Lady's neck and wiped the saliva from her jowls. Luckily his stomach was iron-clad and had gotten past all the drool. Now her tri-color coat was beautiful and her ribs no longer showed.

"Good girl, Lady," he said, praising her for sitting still.

And for not snatching his dinner from his hands.

Lady wagged her tail and panted lightly. Seeing he wouldn't change his mind, she slumped to the floor, gave one last stare and closed her eyes.

The phone rang. Drake glanced at the caller i.d. Larry. They'd just talked—what did he want?

"What's up?" he asked.

"Listen, Drake, you didn't stay long enough to hear this, but Jeremy brought news the Donovans are not the eye of the storm. There's another source. Bigger fish."

Drake planted a foot on the higher rung of the bar stool, his elbow on the counter. "Do you have a name?"

"No. But there's something else you should know about your — "

A door slammed.

Drake had enough surprises to last him a lifetime.

A breathless voice came over the phone. "Larry. Kill. You." Each word rushed out between gasps. "Plane. Today. Six. Not. Packed. Leave. Now." Another door slammed.

"Larry, what about—"

"No time."

"Larry ..." Connection had been severed. Larry style.

Chapter Fifteen

Eric rolled around on a small quilt while Dog lay just out of reach. Mary had adopted the dog when she found it begging by the back door. Since then it had found its way into the home permanently. At six months old, Eric was the biggest heartbreaker around. Eric rolled to his tummy and squealed. The dog's tail thumped from side to side, stopping now and then near Eric's chubby fingers.

Mary rocked with pen and paper in hand.

Eric squealed as he nabbed thin air and rolled over with a huge thump.

Mary's fingers twitched, making two distinct movements. Eric spotted the movement and squealed with delight. Mary caught Selena standing in the doorway and gave a curt nod.

Selena returned the nod, but not the curtness. She'd seen the love in Mary's eyes when no one was looking. She wouldn't push the take-over of Eric.

Mary waved her over.

Selena gently walked over, not wanting to startle Eric since he didn't know her well. She didn't see the toy on the floor until her foot flattened it with a squeak. Dog's head jerked towards the sound and then bolted from the room. Eric didn't respond until his favorite toy of the moment disappeared and then he yelled at the top of his lungs.

Something wasn't right with Eric. If Dog heard, shouldn't he?

Mary shook her head and smiled. She knelt down and crooned an off-key song in his ear and smiled with sadness as Selena stared in bewilderment between the baby and the dog. Mary glanced quickly over at the entry way into the hall and back. Placing a finger to her lips, she made the gesture for quiet. Her eyebrows up, she took both hands, using index fingers only, rolled them over and towards her chest.

Selena didn't understand. Mary grabbed her paper and pen and scrawled a few words.

"Do you sign? ASL?"

She looked at Mary, then Eric, and back again. Eric and Mary were deaf. The only thing she knew how to sign was "thank you." Her fingerspelling wasn't bad if she concentrated.

She fingerspelled, "Fingerspelling only."

Mary smiled and fingerspelled, "Deaf."

Why the secrecy?

As if Mary had read her mind, she fingerspelled, "Andrew wants perfect baby."

It took Selena three times to soak in the letters. She fingerspelled back to her, "Andrew wants a perfect baby?"

Mary nodded once. She fingerspelled, "Eric deaf secret. I can read lips."

"Because of his father?" Selena mouthed, hoping she wasn't over-enunciating the words. She'd heard if one spoke too slowly, it was more difficult for a person who is deaf to understand. "What would happen if he found out?"

Mary took her index finger across her throat.

Damn. Selena not only had to find out who had ordered the hit, but now she had to make sure no one found out about her nephew's deafness.

Double damn.

Eric's gaze alerted both women. Both women sighed with relief in silence when they saw Dog.

Dog padded between the two women as if they didn't exist, plopped down a foot away, his tail went back to an old game between dog and babies. A game both Dog and baby were happy with. The dog was as loyal as they came for pooches. No one called it anything but Dog. Andrew had said, "A dog's a dog. No name.

No tombstone. No engraving needed."

Mary pointed to Dog, slapped her thigh and then snapped her fingers. She pointed to Dog, repeated the movements and gestured for Selena to try. Selena signed dog. Mary shook her head, placed her index on her lips and gestured for her to make the sign smaller.

Several signs later and two diaper changes, the women had found a truce.

*

No one saw Andrew as he watched the two women take on the scene in the middle of the room. Andrew had been kicked in the stomach when he'd laid eyes on her. She wasn't extraordinary in looks, but there was a strength that had shone through her warrior eyes as she'd raced across the square. There had been purpose in her stride yesterday. The intent loud and clear in looks as well as in her hips.

He'd known she hadn't been the one his contact had sent for the interview, but he'd played the cards he'd been dealt. His dearly departed wife owed him. There was more than one way to collect on a debt.

He wanted Selena more than he'd ever wanted anyone. More than he'd wanted Theresa. Theresa had been more waif-like. More in need of protecting. He'd liked that. At first. Then as time wore on, it started getting on his nerves. Her constant whining about everything from his brother's intimidating her in the middle of the night to his father's temper tantrums. His father had protected her far longer than he'd expected him to and in a way that had surprised him. When Theresa had brought Eric into the world, he thought he could love her the way a man loves a woman, but *she* wanted to be first.

His world came first. *He* came first.

Theresa hadn't been able to accept the ranking order of his life.

Then Eric became her number one priority when it should've been him. Even his father doted over Eric.

If his father only knew what was about to come crashing down around his precious empire.

All his life he'd catered to his father's every whim. All of them had. Even his mother, whom he'd loved with all his heart until she'd died. He had placed her on a pedestal, putting her higher and higher when she'd taken the beatings and constant berating from his father without a sound. The day his father told him she'd taken a lover his heart understood she'd needed love. Real love.

He held a loyalty to his father higher than the pedestal he'd placed his mother. He'd watched his mother die slowly, whispering, "My sweet Andrew. I understand, darling. Your mama will always love you." He'd cried for the mother he'd lost. Even at a young age, he'd known it was the reason his father had gained a higher respect for him.

He winced as a cough plunged through the ear piece and into his eardrum.

"Sorry," the voice apologized. "Damn things are too sensitive. I have the report on Selena Malone. You're not going to like the findings," the man on the other end warned. He updated Andrew on what they'd found.

Andrew merely smiled. At least she wouldn't be a complete loss. Someone would be willing to take her off his hands. Killing two birds with one stone provided the best outcome yet.

*

Selena stood over the crib and smoothed the lambs on the soft blanket with her fingertips. Eric had finally fallen asleep, completely innocent of his surroundings.

It had been two weeks since Selena had been paid a nighttime visit by two men. The one she could do without. The other one

... well ... as much as she had wanted to continue with the dream, reality had set in, causing her to wonder if the responses Drake elicited from her were traveling as hot and wicked through his veins. At first she'd caught a glimpse of desire in those dark eyes, and something else. Hurt. Then it was as if he'd sensed the intrusion and shut the emotions down, leaving anger.

The Brahms' Lullaby came to a halt on the CD player attached to the crib's side. She pressed the play and repeat buttons, wondering how much of the lullaby's vibrations Eric would feel. Soon the soothing melody caressed the room, more for a prop in maintaining Eric was a hearing baby. Although she didn't regret coming back to this life for her nephew, she did grieve, deeply, for what should've been. A sister's affection. A mother for her nephew.

Being in Drake's arms.

A shuffling sound from the hallway alerted Selena. She went to the other side of the crib and tucked the covers over Eric's feet.

No one. She glanced down inside the crib one last time. A sound came, so soft it took all her concentration to hear it again. Who was crying?

She hated leaving Eric's side, but the curiosity in her was too hard to ignore. She caressed Eric's cheek. Placing a kiss on her fingertip, she touched his brow. On her way out, she checked the monitor, and then turned the tiny, embroidered pillow hanging from the doorknob to *shhhh*.

Her bare feet guided her down the hall. She stopped at the room next to hers. The crying was faint as she pressed her ear to the door.

"The room's empty."

Andrew's words glided over Selena suspiciously as she faced him.

"I heard someone crying," she answered. Andrew obviously didn't believe her. "I could hear it from Eric's room and tried to follow the sound. It was a woman. I wanted to see if I could help." The smile disappeared at his hard cold stare.

"Your only charge is Eric. Don't worry what goes on behind the other doors."

"I won't stand aside while someone is in distress."

"You will if you value your life," Andrew returned.

The door to her room slammed shut.

She jumped.

Andrew turned away. "Close your window."

"I never opened it." He froze for a second and shook his head as if more to himself than to her words before continuing. "Meet me downstairs in an hour. I'm leaving for a small business trip and would like to see you before I leave."

"Why?" But he'd already taken the corner and had disappeared.

She opened her door and sighed.

On her bed lay her cell phone.

Who had placed it here?

*

Dear Journal,

Don was sitting outside my balcony when I came back to my room. Scared the living daylights out of me with the lights out. Spoke as if he were in another world about a woman crying and babies. He finally popped out of his trance and asked me, point blank, when I was going to have a baby. I couldn't do anything but stare. If he only knew how little time he gave Andrew and me to accomplish that feat. So here I am … wanting to tell him it's none of his business, when he tells me his wife used to sleep in this room with Andrew sleeping next door in the small room off of this one. Then the craziest words came out of the old coot's mouth. I could barely hear him as he whispered, "I wish I coulda kept you alive." Weird doesn't begin to describe what went through my insides.

Big sister, if you ever get married, check into the in-laws, because you never know when you might become the next out-law.

Selena went onto the balcony and stared into the night. She knew she would've laughed if she wasn't here, if her sister wasn't dead, or her nephew wasn't on a hit list, being raised by a murderer. Instead she sank to the floor. The flow of tears came unchecked. She couldn't move. The sadness came in huge waves, one after the other, unrelenting. No sound came from her lips.

A soft, warm breeze suddenly appeared, brushing over her back and hair. The chimes on the balcony teased its player. She closed her eyes, welcoming the soothing touch.

"I can get you out of this."

She wasn't surprised at the sound of his voice or that she hadn't heard him enter. It had always been like that.

"Hello, Drake," she whispered. "You know, I never thought I'd see you again."

He cupped the side of her face and gently wiped the tears with his thumb.

She leaned her head into his touch.

"Is there something you'd like to tell me?" he asked, stilling his caressing.

She knew what he was asking. "What's there to tell?"

"Selena … Open your eyes," he commanded softly.

She shook her head.

"Drake, it isn't safe for you to be in this room. Andrew could come back at any time."

The corner of his mouth lifted to a snarl and a low growl erupted from his throat.

She ignored it. "It's not what you think."

"What then?" he demanded.

"I can't explain."

"You mean won't." He rocked back on the heel of his boots.

The warmth he'd provided moments before vanished. "I'm sorry. I didn't want this to happen," she whispered.

He clenched his hands. "We're married. I honored my part. I

thought you hated deception of any kind."

A knock on the door brought her to her feet and sent him swiftly to the side of the door as it opened.

Mary peeked in and signed, "Goodnight." The door closed.

Drake put his gun back in its place. "You understood that?"

"Yes," she said.

"Well?" He glared across the room.

"Well what?" She smiled as he walked with long strides, remembering another time when he was determined.

"Honey, don't try my patience. Who was that and what did she say?"

"Goodnight."

"Not until you've answered my question."

"Goodnight."

He reached out, hooked her with his arm and brought her close. Old habits were hard to break it seemed. "I'll ask one more time time…"

"You won't have to. Don't be so suspicious of everything," she told him. "Mary is Andrew's housekeeper and she's deaf. She signed goodnight."

He bent his head and breathed deeply as his nose trailed the side of her neck.

"One day you will push me too far, Selena."

He let go of her and strode to the balcony. "I will get the answers I want sooner or later. I just prefer sooner. Though later will work just as well." His eyes took in the top of her hair to the tip of her toes.

"Why are you looking at me in that way?"

"No reason, honey. Just wanted to get one more look at a woman who's traded the living for a dead man."

"It's not like that." She started for him.

In a flash he jumped over the side of the balcony.

"Damn you," she whispered into the wind, looking into the black night.

Chapter Sixteen

Selena wished she'd remembered to grab her robe. If Andrew popped in and looked at her one more time as if he wanted to strip her, she was going to deck him. The thought of him touching her visually, as well as physically, made her ill.

Eric stirred in her arms. His age was one of innocence and wonder. Not knowing the difference between good versus evil was a plus, because every night she spent here was one night too many, creating a harder edge to her heart. It was rocking Eric, the highlight of her days and her nights, that helped to keep her sane and filled with hope that some day the world would change.

She glanced at the angelic face. Mary still wanted her time with Eric and wasn't quite ready to relinquish him into Selena's care completely, but she'd slowly warmed up to her, allowing her to take over most of his care.

Selena longed to take him into her room, fall asleep, and together, they could dream. She shifted Eric to a more comfortable position for both of them.

He flailed his arms and legs, and whimpered.

"Shhh," she crooned. "I'm right here, little one."

"He finally fell asleep?"

Selena nearly jumped out of the rocker. She hadn't seen Andrew standing in the doorway, too engrossed with her own thoughts. He wore black lounging bottoms, his hands tucked inside the pockets.

How long had he been there?

She gave her nephew a smile. "Yeah. Last night was the worst. Hopefully the medication takes root soon. He keeps pulling at his ear."

"Dr. Meldon said the antibiotic would start working within twenty-four hours," he said.

She shivered. He was staring again.

His eyes narrowed. "Are you cold? I could get your robe for you," he offered.

"A little," she answered, untruthfully. If she told him no, then he would get a crazy notion she was attracted or something. Heaven forbid that happened. "But I'd rather not move in case I wake him."

He pulled his hands out of his pockets. "I'd like you to eat with us tonight."

"Eric might need me." Her gut clenched tight at the thought of eating with the family. The first time had been way over the top.

"Be there at six. There's an announcement I want you and the family to hear."

Not a request. An order. Andrew style.

She didn't like it, but she nodded.

*

She was bone tired as she flipped the switch inside her room. A simple black dress lay on the bed. The tags were still on it. Andrew wanted her to wear this and laid it out so she would see it. It was the little things she'd noticed in his controlling personality. She flicked the tag and shrugged at the price. Nothing but the best for this family.

But the best for her was Drake.

She looked at her watch, a present from Larry. Waterproof and dependable. "Just like you," he'd said the day he'd presented it to her. How wrong had he been? Looking back, she hadn't fulfilled any of her obligations.

Familial, business, or marital.

She had an hour to look presentable. She really didn't have time for a shower and it wasn't as though she cared to make an impression, but the need to refresh her mind and body was too hard to resist. She stripped off her sweats and threw them into the hamper. The T-shirt soon followed, along with the cloth Eric had been using as a place to burp on her shoulder.

She closed the bathroom door, dimmed the lights, and adjusted the shower knobs. The room soon filled with steam. She didn't bother turning on the exhaust fan, needing the cloak of steam to give her a sense of privacy and silence. She threw a thick towel over the rim of the etched shower door and stepped into the hot shower. The cascading water massaged her tired body as she leaned against the wall.

She hadn't meant to hold Drake off the entire time. The more he had tried to convince her to go give in, the more she backed away. And the more she wanted him.

And he knew it.

He had been a perfect gentleman, respecting her wishes.

Almost.

She had felt his rein of control starting to slip each night. His hands had skimmed over her as if they would never feel her again. The way his eyes had made a point of meeting hers, his patience thin, had told her time was running out.

She reached for her towel to dry her face. Her hands met the metal rim. "Damn it. I know I put it there."

Despite the warmth of the water a sudden chill swept over her.

A familiar heat soon enveloped her.

"Come here." The voice rough, commanding, thick with desire.

The pull of the heat couldn't be ignored.

She turned, but Drake intercepted, drawing her back.

There was no avoiding him. Not now. She felt safe in his arms. She wanted to forget where she was and why. He pulled her against him and tilted her head back. Hands and water soothed her troubled thoughts, allowing other emotions to surface. He leaned closer, his chin rested on her shoulder as his hands caressed her shoulders, his fingers trailing down her arms.

Her body taut with wanting the touch of his lips, the touch of his hands. His hands paused at her wrists, instantly alerted. As much as she'd teased him in the past, she wouldn't be able hide her need to have him deep inside.

His mouth took control, gliding over her neck, kissing the soft curve of her shoulder as his hands cupped each breast, massaging. She moaned, longing to kiss him. As if he could read her mind, he turned her around and kissed her. His tongue teased and danced with hers. Her fingers trailed, dipping lower. He twined his fingers through her hair and tugged her back.

She looked up, hesitating.

There was no doubt about it. He was in pain. And if she dared, he would retaliate.

Could she handle the consequences?

She dared.

She curled her hand around the length of him and slipped through his hold until she was a breath away. She tasted the tip of him. Tasted the spray of water and sweet heaven.

"Sweet love, don't do it, Selena," he said with a hiss of pain. He pulled her head away, but his hips followed.

She began stroking long and easy, holding the tip of him just inside her mouth, circling it slowly with her tongue. His hips rocked back and forth, his body arched. His hand now held her head closer. Her mouth rocked with him.

"Damn you," he said through gritted teeth. He grabbed her hands and pulled out of her mouth. Lifting her up, he pushed her against the wall. "You're pushing too far. I'd give anything to take you here and now, and if I do, you're leaving with me." He plundered her mouth with his tongue, stroking, kneading her breasts.

She cried against the onslaught of heat. When he stopped, she opened her eyes, realizing his hunger was deeper than her own. The power of his desire shook her. Squirming, she tried pulling free. He held strong. Using his body as an anchor, he held her.

If she had any doubts before, she didn't now. Not with him hard between her legs. The ache below rose to another level, the throbbing sensation painful. Her hips searched for him.

Suddenly her hands were free.

He faced her towards the wall and spread her legs.

Selena struggled to stop him. She couldn't take this constant roller coaster. If he wasn't going to finish what he started, then she was out of here.

She pushed at his hands.

He laughed.

Her body stiffened with outrage at the male tone. "Do you want me to beg?"

He shifted and leaned against her, granting a sense of what was to come but refused to give. His chin touched her shoulder as he whispered into her ear, "How many months, weeks did you have me hanging in your mercy?"

"You knew from the start where I stood." The heat was killing her. What was he waiting for?

She hadn't been a virgin when she'd first met Drake. From the start, he'd been a rock. Steadfast and dependable. And very male. Never had he tried to hide his attraction. At first it had been a simple flirtation and when she'd given him the cold shoulder, he'd taken that as a challenge.

And so had she.

Then she'd fallen for him. Every piece of him.

"Donovan wants you," Drake said, quietly.

Selena sighed.

"Every time you walk into the room, every time you laugh at the baby's antics, every time you crawl into your own little world, he's waiting for the right time to screw you senseless. His slimy hands take every opportunity to touch you and you don't even flinch."

"Don't tell me, hidden cams and mics? Didn't realize that was your style, Drake. Next time I'll remember that."

"Do you like his touch? Do you want him as much as you want me? Because if you do, I'll never touch you again. If you choose him, you can never come back. Never find what could have been. Ask yourself this … Is this small amount of happiness more important than a lifetime? He's a marked man. I know they want him alive, but that's not going to happen."

She reached behind her, eyes still on him, and shut the water off. Sliding the door open, she stepped around him.

"I've thought about this decision over and over again, and I wouldn't change my mind even if I could." She hesitated, as if arguing with herself and pointed to his heart. "It'll give you the answers I can't give you."

He clasped her index within his hand when she would've pulled away.

"This is the last time I ask."

"I know."

Chapter Seventeen

Andrew had lost track of how many times he'd checked his watch. One of his pet peeves was tardiness and she was late. This time he'd allow it, considering he had plenty of time to mold her into the perfect wife, the kind his father would approve of. Old man Donovan thought Eric needed a playmate, another heir to the family business. Although Andrew didn't think the cards were stacked for the future on that subject, he would play along with his father.

A large belch erupted in the air.

His brother, Terrance, was the oldest, but he was the most disgusting piece of garbage around. He thought being the oldest meant coming to the dinner table with his hair uncombed and his shirt unbuttoned. He had refused to wait for everyone to arrive and had started without them.

When his old man was gone, things would change.

Andrew tapped his foot on the tiled floor. What was taking her so long?

Just then Selena breezed in, slightly out of breath. "My apologies," she said.

"We're all allowed one or two indiscretions in this family." He kissed her cheek. "It's the third one you have to worry about."

"I'm really sorry, Andrew," she whispered close to his ear. "I'm afraid the shower relaxed me so much, I lost track of time."

"Not a problem," Andrew said. His arm relaxed a tiny smidgeon after that. "I'm only anxious to make a special announcement and I wanted you to be a part of it."

"I can't wait to hear your news."

Andrew smiled down at her. "You mean *our* news," he said.

Mary came through the door with a tray laden with long-stem glasses filled with champagne. She stopped in front of Andrew. He reached for two and handed one to Selena.

Mary served the rest of the family before melting in the shadows of the next room. Andrew signaled one of the maids to get Mary's attention. The maid touched Mary's arm upon her exit. Mary turned in the direction of the maid's eyes.

"Mary, I'd like you to stay. The last glass is yours," he said, nodded to the lone glass on her tray.

Pleased at how smoothly his plan was running, he raised his glass and began, "Selena, from the moment you entered my sight, I couldn't get you out of my mind. You saved my son's life and mine. Any man would hold onto someone as priceless as you." He turned to the others. "So it is with great pleasure that I announce that Selena and I are getting married."

*

The more Drake watched from their post, the more determined he became. He hadn't got enough of her and couldn't bring himself to leave just yet. Not one drop of emotion was displayed in that beautiful body when he'd said Donovan was a dead man

She'd been complex from the start of their relationship. It had taken him weeks to get more than a cool "no, thank you." Other men had warned him if he wanted more than the friends-only category, he should move onto greener pastures.

But then, he'd never heeded warnings in the past and wasn't about to follow them now. He'd been glad he hadn't, until he'd been left holding the bag.

An empty honeymoon bag.

"Come on, man," Barry growled. "If I have to work with you another twenty-four, I will personally knock you out. The guys have had enough of your moods. You're worse than my mother going through the change."

Drake didn't give a damn right now. Later he would. His plan had already been cemented and couldn't be changed. His gut instinct screamed she wanted out but refused his help.

The front door opened. A beefy giant held the door open and waited. According to Selena's scheduled routine, it was time for the baby's walk.

"Come on. Bring her out," Drake said.

"Patience is a virtue in our game." Barry focused his binoculars.

"When the Agency hired me, it wasn't for my patience."

"You can say that again. Looks like your wait is over."

Selena had put some distance between the slow-moving giant and the black buggy she was pushing. He wanted to take out the man and run with her. The giant was not only checking out their surroundings, but her backside, too.

There were several unanswered questions about some of the inhabitants of that house. The housekeeper had been there before Andrew's mother had been killed and later raised him. They said there wasn't much she could do for Andrew after his mother had been murdered by his father. It was said Andrew had witnessed the action, even held his mother as she died. With his father standing over him, giving no time for privacy, Drake wondered if Andrew had a chance to tell her he loved her.

No one could find anything on the housekeeper. It was as if she didn't exist.

A voice came through his earpiece, "Haven't seen the pup yet, but word is the vet is putting him to sleep. In house clean-up." Then the airwaves went dead.

The word was out. Another hit was taking place.

But who?

Drake felt sorry for the guy if he had to die like his brother but not sorry enough to stop any man connected with the family.

Chapter Eighteen

Someone was following Selena. Someone other than Nate, Andrew's guard. She watched her nephew coo over his toys as they swung from the stroller bar in the gentle breeze.

Eric tried to grab the fuzzy duck and missed. He laughed.

If life were only that simple again, she thought.

The laughter of children reached her. Eric grew silent, his eyes big with wonder as he saw the children running and playing.

Selena leaned over and lifted him into her arms. She smelled his hair, nuzzled his nose with an Eskimo kiss before sitting down on the bench. She enjoyed watching the kids play. Most children were lucky to be oblivious and out of reach of danger's way. There were some who came into the world understanding evil way before their time.

The bench jiggled. Her escort sat next to her. Some mothers had tried to include her in their play dates, but when her escorts glared at them, they kept their distance.

She faced Eric and watched the kids play kickball. "Kiddo, this is as normal as it gets for you and me right now. Soak it in," she whispered. She closed her eyes, wishing she could cry for what could've been but forced the tears back. Someday when they weren't in the thick of danger, she promised silently, more to her sister than Eric, he would know what it was to be safe and loved.

"The ball! Get the ball! He's making it to home," children screamed to a young boy in the outfield. The kicker was already flying to second.

Selena looked up in time to see a kickball flying through the air, landing a few feet away. The outfielder, a small boy, hung back when he saw where it landed. An older boy saw him hesitate and searched for the location of the ball. He glanced at Nate's unsmiling demeanor and the fear in his teammate. The older boy twisted his baseball cap around and headed their way. The kids watched from the field, their faces solemn and filled with wonder at the older boy's guts in retrieving their ball.

Each step closer, she noticed he was a young adult rather than a boy. The young man stood in front of the ball.

Nate didn't touch the ball or make an offer to. It was as if he dared him to be a man. The kid squared his shoulders, his eyes hard. Unspoken words between kid and man were loud and clear. It was a warning. Plain and simple.

Nate gave a curt nod. The kid did the same.

Eric laughed, breaking the ice for a moment, drawing attention to him. Nate and the kid turned and smiled at Eric's antics. Just as quickly, they lost their smiles. The kid picked up the ball. Deliberately, he took his time, showing, he didn't give a damn who Nate was or who he worked for.

The young outfielder waited eagerly for the ball. His hero whispered something into his ear and ruffled his hair.

Selena knew she wasn't the only one taking this all in. Other mothers watched the scene unfold. She didn't have to look in their eyes. She saw it everyday she came to the park. She heard their whispers, saw the nods and pointing to the bulge under Nate's jacket. The Donovans were well-known in this area.

And even though Eric was an innocent babe, they wanted nothing to do with this family.

Nate didn't look at her. "I'm not an ogre. But the kid wouldn't have allowed me to give it to him. He knows I'm bad news. My luck he'll go into a profession which could cause downsizing in my job."

Nate's eyes were unreadable. It was as if he wished he were anywhere but here. "The kid has guts. A few years older and he could command big money in my field. In the old days, Don would've forced a kid like that to work for him, using any means necessary. Real or trumped up. He made sure he had the resources available to follow through. I've seen it."

She caressed Eric's hair as Nate spoke. She kind of felt sorry for Nate, but not enough to forget he was paid by the Donovans. He was in for life. Eric was the one who suffered. Eric didn't have his mother's arms around him at this moment.

She sensed rather than saw him.

Drake was here.

For how long, though?

She didn't dare case the area, even casually. Her normal routine always focused on the baby. It had always been her alone time without cameras, family, and danger lurking around. Here it was minimized. If she went against her routine, Nate would sense something was up and inform Andrew.

The sooner she got through to Drake that he would jeopardize her position, the safer Eric would be.

"Nate, would you hold Eric while I run to the ladies' room? I think it's that time of the month." She didn't give him a chance to deny her request or care that a hard man like Nate would be embarrassed. She placed Eric in his arms, a bottle in his hands, and hurried towards the ladies' room.

If Drake had followed her here, he would know where she was going. She didn't know if she should feel irritation at such a close eye on her activities or pleasure for his offer of help.

Two women came out as she entered the bathroom. The stalls were empty. No voices outside the entrance. She gripped both sides of the white enamel sink, aged with rust and lack of care, and studied the rings under her eyes.

"I can make those disappear," Drake said, his voice smooth as silk.

Looking past her image in the mirror, she found him watching her from the end of the stalls, wearing black shades and a three-day growth.

"Shouldn't you take care of your own first?" she asked.

"I tried, but she wouldn't let me. This time she won't have a choice."

"A woman can take care of herself, you know."

He gave a dry laugh and smiled. "Jumping from love and respect to this? Try again, honey."

Until he found his way into her bedroom, she'd been able to suppress her emotions. There was no turning back. She'd made her decision and needed complete control for however long this took.

"I'm a very strong, resourceful woman, Drake."

"Apparently."

It didn't matter his tone was anything but complimentary. She knew it was the pain hidden behind the shades. "There's something about my life I haven't told you."

"That's obvious."

Hands on hips, she faced him, her smile humorless. "What's obvious is you have a few things you haven't let out of the bag yourself."

He came out of the shadows, stopping when he was close enough to touch, but didn't. "We'll have time for a game of questions and answers soon," he whispered.

A faint scraping on the concrete brought her to her senses.

She turned, but Drake stalled her, holding her by the arm. "Now," he commanded.

She tried getting in stance to ward off whatever he had planned.

She felt a tiny prick on her arm. It was too late. Whatever had been injected was working fast. Light-headed and woozy, it was all she could do to stand.

A man's hands circled around her waist.

"Don't touch her."

The hands left and another took their place. Gentle and caring. Drake's.

She had no choice but lean on Drake. Laying her head on his shoulder, she whispered, "You don't understand. The baby needs me."

His arms were no longer soft and yielding. "The Donovans take care of their own."

*

Selena rubbed her eyes. Her tongue felt pasty and her head ached. It was way past Eric's waking time. She needed to get moving. She sat up on the edge of the bed, feeling every muscle, every bone in her body protest at the movement. It was then she remembered the park and Drake.

"Dammit, Drake. You don't know what you've done," she whispered. "If you only knew."

Someone knocked on the door. She didn't bother responding. They would come in anyway.

The door opened. The man entered, looked her over with a quick glance. "Drake will be back shortly. Are you hungry?"

Her stomach lurched at the thought of food. "Where are we?"

"Hotel." He surveyed the hallway before closing the door and bolting it.

"I don't know who you are or what your place is in all of this, but you shouldn't have taken me. Who are you?"

"Does it matter?"

"Not particularly, but wouldn't you prefer to give me a name instead of letting me make one up?"

The man gave a short laugh. "Barry."

Selena needed to stretch her legs and stood up.

"Why shouldn't we have taken you? What Drake wants, Drake gets."

"I need this job."

"You weren't happy with your previous lifestyle?"

"Ahh … that's right. A friend of Drake's. I'm glad he has friends like you. To answer your question, yes, I was happy. There's someone who needs me more."

She walked to the window and peeked through the curtain. Barry moved her away and closed it, but not before she caught a glimpse of a Donovan car patrolling the parking lot. Apparently, they hadn't gone too far. If she could convince Barry to let her go without giving away her position … She didn't have to look at Barry to know he would be as unyielding as Drake.

If Larry hadn't told anyone she was back in, and Drake was oblivious to her past, then Barry was in the dark as well. His gun was holstered and he had placed himself back at the door.

She rubbed the center of her forehead with her fingertips and closed her eyes.

"Are you okay?"

"I'm fine. Just a little woozy."

She took another step. Her feet faltered and she swayed.

"You need to sit down and rest."

She swayed some more and crumpled. Barry was by her side instantly. He gathered her into his arms and placed her on bed. She drew her knees to her chest and moaned. He felt her forehead.

Taking both legs, she kicked at his chest and grabbed his gun. Selena was on top of him the moment he hit the ground. He opened his eyes and found his own gun staring at him.

The hammer clicked back.

"I want your clothes on the bed now," she ordered. "I'm not screwing around. Now."

She gathered the clothes and motioned Barry to the bathroom. She aimed her gun at the tub. "Get in, face down."

"Drake won't stop," Barry said, complying.

She hesitated at the door. "I know that better than anyone." And closed the door.

She aimed a few kicks at the doorknob. The knob fell to the floor. She checked his clothing, found his cell phone and an extra clip. Hoping the window wasn't painted shut, she pushed. The window slid open. As she climbed onto the fire escape and threw the clothes over the side, the black sedan turned the corner.

She tucked the gun and clip under her shirt, before jumping to the pavement. The car stopped as she ran. The passenger door opened. She slid in next to Tony.

Tony gave her cursory glance. "What happened to your shoulder?"

She looked. Her shoulder was bleeding. Probably gouged it on the fire escape. "I'll be fine."

She checked the side mirror. No Barry or Drake in sight. "This isn't setting well with Mr. Donovan."

Andrew and his father were suspicious types. Even though she'd flagged Tony down, they'd still see it as a betrayal. As would Drake. But all she could focus on right now was Eric.

The house was quiet as Selena entered the side door. Mary's eyes were scrunched as if worried. When she saw Selena, she mumbled something and hurried into the kitchen.

Senior and Junior had to be on the warpath. Old Man Donovan ranting and raving of betrayal unlike Andrew, who kept it to himself. She preferred senior Donovan's style over Andrew's. One never knew what to expect from the quiet ones.

She turned the shower to the hottest setting. Steam filled the room. Once her clothes were off, she tossed them in the trash can. A thick, over-sized towel heated on the bar behind her. She pulled it off and wrapped it around her. The heat provided the comfort she needed to maintain. And ready herself for whatever the Donovans directed her way.

She closed the door behind her as she left the bathroom, preventing the therapeutic steam from escaping. Gathering the essentials she needed, she headed back. The nursery door was open. Normally, she kept it closed. As she pulled it, she saw Andrew.

He was staring outside, hands in his pockets. He didn't acknowledge her, choosing the outside view. "I wish it hadn't happened. Just as I wish this isn't happening." This time he faced her. "You look beautiful, by the way. I promise they'll be discreet where it'll be placed," Andrew said as he strode past her, stopping long enough to glide his fingers over her shoulder.

What he meant by that would be known soon enough.

The door opened behind her. She heard him talking. Thinking he had more to say this time, she turned.

Six of Andrew's men were planted in her room.

Her towel slipped. She grabbed it before it revealed too much. It was all she could not to go into shock.

"Keep her dignity. And hide it. It's her first one. Hopefully, her last. Remember I detest screaming. Unless ..." She knew he what he was about say: *I'm inside her.*

She wouldn't beg or plead her case. It didn't matter if she was innocent of betraying him. It was his way of saying, "Should they try again ... keep your mouth shut."

Three of the goons advanced. There was no place to run or hide. They circled around her and motioned towards the bed.

She couldn't move. She'd seen what damage the soldering gun could do.

Two men positioned around the bed. One at the side. The other at the foot of the bed. It was the man on the other side she couldn't stop staring at. He was holding the small gun in his hand as though it was nothing.

Every instinct within her screamed. Fight took over where flight couldn't. As the three men hauled her over to the bed, she began kicking and screaming, not caring her towel had dropped. One leg connected with a chest, another to a softer area.

"Don't hit her. Andrew will kill you."

They tossed her on the bed, the men, who had positioned around the bed, grabbed her arms and legs, flipped her over and held her down. She thrashed from side to side until someone sat on her legs and shoved her shoulders down, holding her from further movement.

Something warm touched her buttock.

She screamed over and over as the man continued the slow motion on her skin. She tried bucking her captor off and pushed at the others, but they were stronger.

A phone rang.

Someone answered it. Then someone placed a hand over her mouth. Unable to withstand the pain, she passed out.

*

Selena sat up and fell back down when a hot searing pain from her buttocks raged loud and strong. She bit back a cry.

Soft clucking came from beside her. Fingers soothed her forehead while another hand pushed her gently back. Mary now sat on the bed, checking her over.

Mary shook her head.

"Why are you — " Selena began, but was interrupted by a shake Mary's head, her finger at her lips as she stared pointedly at the lamp.

Selena followed Mary's eyes. Mary glanced from Selena to the lamp again, shaking her head.

Mary signed, "Are you okay?"

"The pain is killing me," Selena signed back, emphasizing the amount of pain by using facial expressions. "Where's Eric?"

"Sleeping."

"You need to get as far away as you can," Mary signed.

"What about Eric? You?"

"Eric is safer here. I can't leave."

"Eric has a contract out on him."

Mary jerked back but managed to veil it quickly. Her facial expression mirrored the face of a seasoned poker player. "Who are you?"

"The same as you. A marked woman."

Mary pulled her hair back, revealing a vertical scar.

Chapter Nineteen

Instantly Mary's hand traced it. "It's old. From another time."

"I know it's the trademark of the Donovans. You knew they were marking me." Selena moved to a semi-sitting position, grimacing at the pain in her backside.

The hardness in Mary's eyes couldn't hide the heartache. "I know this house has more secrets and ghosts than the White House. Including you. I can't leave now and neither can Eric. The pieces will fall into place soon enough."

"I can protect Eric."

Mary went to the door and stopped. "So can I. I have more leverage than the Agency and your frustrated male friend. Even the ghost has more leverage than you do at this moment."

"Have you seen her?"

"Heard." Mary laughed. "Sorry. I'm not laughing at you, but I — Never mind. I'll rephrase that. Felt the vibrations. There are so many women brought into this house. Their screams. Their terror. Their ecstasy. Not in that order, but none of it escapes this house."

After Mary had left, Selena slipped off the bed, wincing at the pain. She needed Mary's help in pulling Eric out of here. She pulled the drapes aside and took in the expanse of Donovan's estate. He had everything a man could possibly want. And yet ... he still wanted more.

Opening the French doors, she stood in the archway, allowing the wind to blow over her. The aroma of Moon flowers caressed the room. Sometimes she would catch the anguish in Andrew's eyes before he quickly masked it whenever he saw her looking. Those were the only times she had any sympathy for him. It made him more human. Almost child-like.

She glanced at the rocking chair. As if Theresa's ghost knew she had questions, the rocker began moving, aided by the wind.

What would Old man Donovan's wife have told Theresa?

"If only you were alive," she said.

The rocking became stronger as the wind played with the chair. She knelt beside it. Tracing the intricate designs on the spindles, she noticed they weren't like anything she had ever seen before. She'd remembered something Mary had mentioned about Gracie, Don's wife, who had a love for carving before marriage.

"Of course," Mary had said, "Don put the kibosh on the hobby. He felt Gracie's only priority should be making babies for him. Don had this chair commissioned especially for Gracie. When Andrew married Theresa, he thought she would like the idea of it being one of a kind. Handmade. Gracie wanted to carve the chair and pass it on to her first born."

Mary had told her Gracie found a way to carve, placing her signature on the chair Don hadn't been too observant when he thought he'd gotten his own way. He wanted everything his.

Selena gently tilted the chair on its side. There was only one place Don would never see Gracie's signature mark.

And there it was, underneath.

Gracie singed into the wood.

The irony made her smile. An outright refusal to bow to the Donovan.

If Gracie was as smart as Selena thought she was, she would do more than make her mark. Selena righted the rocker and quickly retrieved the reading magnifying glass she'd found from the nightstand drawer. Taking a closer look, she studied the swirls and curves of the spindles. Not quite sure if what she was seeing was her imagination or real, she started from the top of each spindle. Her hands shook. The only way she could possibly be sure was if she took pictures of each of the spindles and laid them out, because she knew if she didn't, not only would she die of curiosity, but when she left, the rocker would not be available for any more inspections. That rocker and her sister's journal could be the leads the Agency has been looking for.

She went into the closet and pulled out what looked to be a pen but which was really a digital camera Larry had provided. She snapped for at least fifteen minutes. She could download them later for studying. Luckily, computer technology had come a long way in allowing the pictures to be enlarged without distorting them. She pulled the tiny disk from the camera and placed it in the port on the side of her watch.

Someone sighed.

Selena whipped around.

No one.

*

Andrew hated having his future bride marred, but ... that was life. The urge to show her who was in charge had hit him strong and hard. If she was anything like his departed wife, she'd fight him tooth and nail. The little slut of a dead wife had preferred someone else over him.

His phone rang. "Yes?" He listened. No pleasantries. Straight to the point.

"My office. Now," the other voice barked.

His father had just summoned him for the third time this day. He was tired of being his father's lackey. His father's ideal power leaned towards totalitarian. Every night dear ol' daddy couldn't stop hounding him for more grandchildren. The more bloodlines that followed, the more bloodshed he could dictate.

If only his father knew what the future held.

His mouth curled with hatred for the secrets he held and an inability to control certain things in his life which accounted for last night.

*

Drake slammed his fist into the door frame. Son of a bitch. He was trying to protect her. She did not know the full extent of the Donovans' merciless torture and he was not about to lose someone else he loved to them—and so he had arranged to grab her while she was on her daily outing with the child. It wasn't a total surprise she had escaped or that Barry had underestimated her. He had done the same.

He would not make that mistake again.

*

Selena found Mary in the kitchen.

Mary signed, "I know what you're thinking, but it's impossible. Andrew has too many eyes. Go tell Eric goodbye."

"I can't leave without Eric. If he stays, I stay." Selena's signs were still awkward, but improving. At least Mary had stopped cringing when she tried. She'd learned the hard way one wrong motion, placement or facial expression could create a far different meaning than what she had intended.

"I can't protect both of you and I'm sure Eric would be your first choice." Mary turned Selena towards the door and edged her out. "If you try to take Eric out of here, I will take you down myself."

What the hell was going on? Was Mary on her side or the Donovans'?

"Honey, if you take Eric with you, you'll make things worse. The lessons of time need to finish unraveling. There's more going on than you realize."

"How much more?"

"There's not enough time to go into it now. Go say goodbye to Eric. In three days, I'll text the Blackberry I placed in your bag. If you don't receive a text, then we're either in hiding and it's not safe to contact you or we're dead. If I don't hear from you within five minutes after texting, I'll assume you can't and go on. We're going into hiding for as long it takes. All communication ties will be broken forever."

"You can't keep Eric away from me forever!" she signed vehemently. "I won't let you. He's my nephew—" Selena stopped but it was too late. She'd revealed her true identity.

"I know. Your sister had a picture of the two of you from high school. It was the only picture she had of her family."

Selena froze.

"Your identity is safe with me. If they find out, you are both dead. Then Eric will never know his family."

"How will he know he has family if you've hidden him away?"

"Oh, he'll know."

"And you know this because ..." She was being sarcastic and didn't care.

Andrew entered the side door. "I see you've developed another talent during your spare time." Mary faced him as he tapped her arm. "I want every word. Now."

"Selena is your deceased wife's sister."

Andrew listened with cold, deadly silence. "You haven't told me anything new." He focused on Selena. "I've been waiting for you to contact me ever since your sister died. Poor thing. Cut down in her prime. It's too bad she didn't live to see her son's first steps."

It took every ounce not to rip his throat out.

"If you hadn't come along, I would've hunted you down. Your sister owes me a son. Unfortunately, the 'until death do us part' came sooner than expected."

"You have Eric," she reminded him.

His smile didn't reach the darkness of his eyes. "My child should have the opportunity of experiencing the same motherly love as any kid."

Eric wasn't his child. The idea sent a shockwave through Selena. What if Theresa had taken a lover . . . and Eric was that man's child, not Andrew's? And what if Andrew knew it? Or suspected it?

He hauled her by the arm, yanking her towards the stairs.

Selena twisted and signed as he ignored her attempts to escape, not caring if she wasn't looking where she was heading. "Why?" she asked Mary. Selena stumbled as her foot hit the back of the first step.

Andrew didn't stop.

She barely caught Mary's signs before she faced the other direction so she wouldn't break her neck. Mary's facial expression was nonexistent, betraying no emotion whatsoever as she signed, "For Eric's safety."

How the hell was it for Eric's safety?

She felt her hair being ripped from the roots as Andrew yanked on her.

"Dammit! Let go! I can walk up the stairs without any help." She jerked away, trying to get her body positioned to attack, but he held fast.

"A gentleman always helps a lady up. I wouldn't want my father to think he had raised his son without manners." At the top he turned towards a still on-looking Mary. "My future wife won't be taking care of Eric tonight. Or tomorrow. In fact," he added. "Until you hear from me, you're in charge of Eric's needs. Do not let my fiancé near her nephew."

Selena was released.

His hand strayed to her shoulder, the touch light, but deceptive as he shoved hard.

If it weren't for her quick reflexes, she would've hit the wall and unable to protect herself.

"What happened to the gentleman?" she bit out, no longer willing to placate his rising temper.

When Selena tripped over the last stair, she doubled over. He released the death grip on her hair and for a moment the sweet release from the pain was too much to bear. Freedom was short-lived as his hand latched onto the collar of her blouse and dragged across the floor of the hallway. She reached behind, scratching, nailing him with her claws. Anything for air.

"You're choking me," she rasped out.

He tightened his hold.

She twisted and kicked.

He kicked her in the stomach.

She couldn't breathe. Slipping two fingers in between her skin and collar allowed her enough air into her lungs for the strength to maneuver her legs between his. She didn't care what she connected with. She only knew she had to try anything. She rammed straight up.

He went down.

She rolled but not in time. The heavy weight prevented further escape.

"You stupid, little bitch," he said through his teeth. "You're going to wish I put a bullet through your empty head."

"Like hell. You had my sister killed. Now you want to kill your own son."

He was dead weight, his breathing ragged. "I didn't place the hit on Eric. I have bigger plans for the like of the kid. He's perfect for the market and will bring the most secluded bidders out of hiding."

"Sell your son on the black market to another family? You're kidding me, right?"

"Andrew, we need to talk," a man said behind them.

Andrew hesitated.

Selena had seen the man before. He was called the godfathers of godfathers, known little for his mercy, but the brief emotion she caught in his eyes had mercy and sorrow.

Andrew nodded, then met her look dead on. The last thing she heard him say before his fist connected with her jaw, "There's more to slavery than women."

*

When she woke up, she found herself with a splitting headache, no clothes, and chained to the bed. What a helluva way to wake up. She had no way of knowing how long she'd been out. She gave the chain a small tug, not wanting to alert Andrew she was awake. A small current of electricity met her resistance.

She bit her lip, jerking her arms in response.

A stronger current wave seared her flesh.

She cried out when she met wave after wave as she tried avoiding the chains.

"Do you like?" Andrew asked from the nursery.

Something wet trickled down her lip. She tasted the blood. Resisting the urge to show weakness, she ignored it and forced her body not to react.

He stayed in the dark shadows. "One of my online bidders graciously shared this parlor trick. Each time you move, the current becomes stronger until you either die of a heart attack or you stop trying to get away."

The shadow had moved to the balcony. From the moonlight, she could detect he was holding something in his hands. He wore only lounging bottoms. "Though I suspect, and hope, your willpower holds out, allowing a very special bidder to pay extra for your, shall we say … spirit."

He dropped his pants and walked into the light.

She knew she should've trusted Drake with her past, but she thought the past would never resurface. If she'd allowed Drake that wedding night, then she could've pulled it from her memories to help her through the night.

He climbed on the bed and straddled her hips. One hand stroked her hair. "I'm sorry. He made me do it, but you left me with him." His hands trailed her arms and chest. "All I ever wanted was your protection and his love. Instead, you left me with images a child should never have to sleep with."

She didn't see his other hand until it was too late, pulling away before she could stop herself. Pain and electrical waves flooded her mind and body. He felt it, too. His body jerked with each convulsion, riding it out.

He laughed and held a cold object close to her hip, flipping her part way, not caring if she was engulfed in pain. He wanted to touch the mark he had ordered his men to place on her. He traced the mark.

She heard a click. Cold metal touched her backside. She flinched, though not enough to attract a current. She broke into a cold sweat at the metal warming against her skin. The warmth seared with ferocity.

He sighed. "I forgot to mention any kind moisture creates a continuous flow to your body."

She couldn't stop her body from moving away from the heat or the sweat. She screamed in pain at the electrical currents rolling in wave after wave. She tried bucking him off, but the last bolt of electricity pushed her past her limit. She screamed every obscenity, not caring anymore who heard her.

It took every ounce of control not call out for Drake.

Chapter Twenty

Barry watched Drake tensely. They could hear Selena's screams. Through his underground spies, Andrew knew they were out there and he enjoyed baiting his enemies.

Drake started to scale the wall. Barry expected that and went after him.

"Drake. Dammit. Get a grip. You can't help her right now."

Drake threw a punch.

Barry shoved Drake against the wall, throwing a right cross. At Barry's signal, a colleague hit Drake from behind.

Drake hit the ground, face down.

A man dressed in fatigues, his face hidden by the dark and paint, grabbed Drake's arms while Barry took hold of his feet. Both men dragged him over to the wall, propping him against it. Barry signaled. The man crouched next to Drake, his rifle between his legs.

Barry hated hearing any woman crying, but if Drake ran in there with his heart instead of his head, they'd all die. He had a date when this was all over. Damned if Drake was going to ruin it a second time.

*

Selena felt every vibration run through her. Her body couldn't react. It was exhausted and close to giving out.

"I see you're still with me. How remiss of me not to offer you a drink." Andrew poured water into a glass. He held it to her lips. "Would you like some?"

She couldn't answer. She could only wait to see what he would do next. It wasn't long. She felt the glass at lips. Water came sparingly. She opened her mouth wider to accept more.

The glass disappeared. She received more water. Just not in her mouth. He threw it at the chains on her wrists. Pain engulfed her with each shock. He waited. The pain lessened when the water dried.

Until he did it again.

She didn't hear the door open.

Or see Andrew falling on the floor.

Someone soothed her pain with soft strokes across her forehead. "Shhh. It's okay. Your man will be here shortly. I need to take care of Andrew before he does something he regrets even more. I made a promise to him and I intend to keep it."

*

Selena needed to use the bathroom but if she asked to go, Andrew would only delight in watching her urinate all over herself, laughing at the double effect it would cause with the electrical current.

"Do you need to go to the bathroom?"

Selena rolled away from the voice but rolled back when she remembered the pain the movement could bring. It was then it was noticed the chains had been taken off. She curled up in a ball, lifting her head to put a face to the words.

"You're one helluva lady," Barry said. "Even though you ruined my date, I'd pick you to back me up any day."

A door shut across the room.

Selena lay there not caring she was naked. A blanket covered her body.

"I'll take her to the bathroom."

Drake.

"I can do it myself," she told him. It dawned on her they were no longer in Andrew's home, but another place entirely.

When Barry left, Drake leaned over. "You scared the hell out of me. Do you know they had to sedate me with the butt of a rifle to stop me from coming in after you?" He uncovered her arms, inspected the damage, then covered them up, switching to her legs. He took her into the bathroom and set her on the commode. Turning his head to give her privacy, she used his body as a crutch, unwillingly. When she finished, he set her in a waiting tub of warm, scented water.

She began to cry, the tears and pain racked her body.

He picked up a wash cloth and poured lavender scented soap on it. He gently held her arm at the elbow, cradling it with his arm. He washed it and then the other. He did the same with her legs.

She stopped shaking, though the tears still fell silently, as she allowed him to take care of her. He guided her deeper into the tub as he held her neck, washing her hair with the same scented soap. When he was sure she could cry no more, he washed her face.

He opened a large towel and enfolded her into it and into his arms. He cradled her in his lap, gently drying her. Carrying her back to the bed, he laid her down and covered her back up.

*

It didn't take long for Selena to fall asleep. Leaning up on his elbow, Drake watched her sleep. He brushed the hair away from her eyes, the hair slightly damp from her tears. Her killer smile wasn't the first thing he'd noticed about her that day in the coffee shop. It was the long eyelashes and the way she stared straight through him as if she were sizing him up. Then she walked away from him, declining the coffee and the date.

The men standing around at the newspaper counter had smirked. The moment he'd arrived in that forsaken town, rumors floated around about the ice in her veins. The men, who'd tried and been shot down, placed bets on those who were making a move to ask her out. He never gave credence to rumors, but he had been willing to put it to the test.

Her smile knocked everyone for a loop with the attitude attached to it. When she'd directed it his way, he was hit hard. He knew she had a penchant for caramel mocha lattes from the weeks he'd been there. When he'd ordered it at the counter and carried it over, he'd caught the slight hesitation.

He had never seen her do that with anyone. When he looked closer, he saw the reaction he had on her. The slight dilation of her pupils, the slight hitch of breath. The biting of her lip.

She'd eyed the caramel oozing out of the cup, her tongue caressing the edge of her lips.

He had longed to taste her lips, her mouth.

It had taken him two weeks for her to accept a cup of coffee from him. Now they were back to square one.

She didn't trust anyone.

Especially him.

He never thought he'd hurt the way he had the day she'd left him. It wasn't the wedding night he was after like she'd thought. It was the idea of watching her sleep next to him. Her laughter. Her teasing. Her determination. She had never experienced his determination. He'd enjoyed the bantering, the sexual overtones, but if he really hadn't wanted to wait for their wedding night, he could've put on the charm. Out of respect for her, he'd waited, goading her into the playfulness.

Hearing the terror-filled screams in the night winds from her room would haunt him forever. After he'd found his brother, he'd thought the hate boiling inside had been the worst he could feel. Until Andrew hurt her. He didn't know why Selena was with Andrew, but he bet Larry knew.

Drake reached for his phone.

Taking him by surprise, Selena rolled over and latched her arms around his chest, sighing as she rubbed her cheek against his chest.

He decided Larry could wait.

*

Selena woke in the darkness and froze. A man's arm held her. Terror rose, cutting off her breath, then stilled at the memory of Drake bathing her.

"I can't believe you even think you're going back there." He drew her on top of him.

She made circular motions on his chest with her fingertips. She didn't have a choice in looking at him, not when he held her by the shoulders, stalling her attempts at avoidance.

"Drake, what do you want me to say?"

"You can say whatever you want but it doesn't matter. You're not thinking straight, so one of us has to be rational."

She rolled from him. "You don't know what's at stake," she hissed at him. "If I don't do this, it will haunt me for the rest of my life."

"Seeing you in those chains, drenched from Andrew's warped sense of foreplay with electrical current will haunt me. You don't have a clue how bad things were going to get. He had cameras in the room, webcamming for his private buyers, and while you fought and hung on, the numbers on the website skyrocketed each time you screamed. Each time you woke up. Each time you threatened to kick his ass. And when you cried out to him that you would never give in, the numbers tripled."

"You were out there."

"Everyone at the Agency thinks you're a traitor. If Mary hadn't helped, you would be dead."

*

For two days Selena had slept and for the first time since she'd left him on their wedding day, Drake relaxed. He was tired of not having a normal life. And most of all he wanted his wife safe in his arms for the next fifty years. He could only imagine Larry, grieving for his daughter who'd disappeared. He had Selena back. He had no intention of letting her go again.

Her long legs were twisted in the sheet. Bruises had appeared around her wrists and ankles from the chains.

"Don't look at me like that. I had to do it. It's the only way." She stretched cat-like, pulling the sheet around for modesty.

"Am I to understand that you intend to go back?" he asked, placing his drink on the nightstand.

She cradled her head in her hand, slightly grimacing as she added weight to her wrist. "I was told I had to play this all the way through. There is no other way. I'm branded in more ways than one."

"We'll see about that. I want a name," he demanded, stilling the tracing her free hand was making on the bed.

He tipped her chin up and waited.

"Why?"

"So I can kill him."

She moved, but he held firmly. "Then I wouldn't have a husband."

"I'll always be your husband."

"Not if the Agency sentences you to death for killing Larry."

A murderous expression briefly crossed over him. The silence deadly.

"What are you saying?"

"I have my orders," she said. She rolled to the other side before he could stop her, wrapping the sheet around her as she did.

"There's a side of me you haven't seen. I will not have my wife placing herself in danger." He gave her a look as she started to speak. "Your involvement in the Agency is in the past and it will stay in the past from here on out. Screw the Agency."

She brushed past him. Intentionally.

It wasn't a dare but a battle of wills. It was her way of announcing he hadn't seen a certain side of her either.

Chapter Twenty-One

Story Time poked her head out of her stall as Selena approached. Horses and barn, strong from the summer heat, greeted her. She raised her hand slowly so the Appaloosa wouldn't shy away. Her fingers brushed the glossy coat, loving its softness. Story Time was green broke and gentle as a kitten. The barn, used as a boarding front, had six other stalls of various breeds and all of them were raring to go out. She'd only been here for a few days and for the length of time she spent out in the barn, it was easy to recognize which were touchable.

But then, what else did she have to do? Being held prisoner against her will had left her with too much time on her hands. And her mind. Story Time jerked her head to one side and snorted.

Liquid lightning shot straight down to the heart of her libido.

"I hear him, too." She knew it was bound to happen sooner or later. Being in each other's company day and night was becoming harder and harder. Especially during the nights when sleep eluded her, knowing he slept next to her. Life had a way of mocking her self-imposed celibacy.

She heard the sound of his boots on the sawdust covered flooring. But then, he wasn't trying to be silent. He had been waiting for the right time.

He should've forgotten her.

Knowing he was near and intended to fulfill that promise he'd made stirred up long forgotten sensations, threatening to rack her body.

It stole her breath away.

Behind her, his breathing came out in short clips. The tension in the air tight, his emotions held by a tight rein.

She fought the urge to buck, wanting to run. To fight the

inevitable. Her heart refused to comment, scared by the emotions running high through her. The adrenaline between her legs had paralyzed her instinct to flee. It wasn't that any man would do. Against everything she was fighting, she still wanted him. There were so many questions to be answered, so many plays to be played out before either of them could take the time it deserved to see where this would lead.

He didn't trust her.

And she certainly didn't trust him.

He wanted answers.

Answers that she couldn't give him, because she doubted he'd believe them.

But there was one thing she did know. This afternoon he wasn't thinking about the mission. He was being led by his desire to have what he wanted. What should've been his that night after the ceremony.

Their wedding night.

Even though it meant one of them might not make it out of this mission, he would make his claim on her.

He stopped a few feet behind her. There was no doubt he was at his limit in waiting for to acknowledge what she'd cheated them from having.

*

Drake watched the smooth, steady strokes of her fingers. Each movement controlled. Too controlled. Which was a sure sign she was going to fight the inevitable. That night he'd brought her here, he'd been caught up in his own fury, fighting the urge to strangle the first person he came in contact with who was connected with the Donovan family. The woman he knew was hot blooded and loved to push his buttons. Despite the heat coiled within him for months, he'd been willing to wait until after the ceremony.

And now, she was mixed up with the Donovans.

Living with them either meant the woman he had first met had hidden the arctic ice from him or the fire had been suppressed.

Because he sure as hell never got a chance to stoke that fire.

Until now.

He didn't know what kind of hold Donovan had over her and part of him didn't care. He only knew the day she stopped being one of them was the day they'd place the last mark of deception.

The day she'd draw her last breath.

He wanted her out of the organization. He shook pictures of the future from his mind. The possibility of seeing her dumped somewhere like his brother was too much. The demons of hate clawed at his soul, urging him to walk away, screaming to be released.

Yet, the only thing clawing to the surface was need.

The need to lick every part of her.

He took a step back and forced himself to stay. They were both trying too hard to fight the attraction.

"Turn around," he told her quietly. She continued to stroke the horse's neck.

"Why not accept the inevitable?"

Her hand stopped, quivering, in mid-stroke.

"Two reasons. One," she said, with quiet determination "Why should I? I didn't ask to become your exclusive play toy. And two, you don't want me to."

"You still feel it. I know I certainly do," his voice thick with wanting her. "If you'd turn around — "

He didn't have to continue, the insinuation was enough. "You're cross," she told him, her tone biting and full of contempt.

He hated talking to her backside. If they were going to stay like this, he preferred communicating in other ways. "But at least I'm honest. It's more than you can say."

She was too reserved, too quiet. What was she planning?

Escape was impossible. She had no way of knowing their location. He had a man posted every mile from the roadway to the property line and ten armed guards milled around the property inside and outside twenty-four-seven. No one could slip in or out unnoticed.

"If you want to play this out, the ending will be the same whether we do it your way or mine. Realize that it'll be my name screaming out of those gorgeous lungs. Not his," he rasped.

She did turn around then, her body straight, rigid with pride, her eyes flashed angrily at him. "It can't happen."

"As we speak, he's a dead man."

Anguish replaced the fire in her eyes. "For your sake, I hope you fail."

She spoke so low, he barely heard that. From past reports, Andrew's women and the unspeakable crimes were many. So, why would she choose Andrew over him?

His body pulsed with high energy at the thought of pushing her to the point of no return.

He wanted her hot and willing.

*

Selena stared at the hardness in his eyes. She couldn't tell him that he was everything Andrew wasn't. That he was more a human being. More of a man.

That would create more problems. She hated to be a part of this, being on the wrong side.

You can't change the direction of life once it's in progress, she told herself. If only life hadn't stolen her sister. She would've tried to find other ways of protecting Theresa. Called in favors. Anything to get her sister to safety. How she hated herself at this moment. She hated her reasons for what she'd done and for what she planned to do. There was too much at stake.

Something more precious than her own life.

Drake's love and Eric's life.

Drake hadn't moved. Despite the heaviness of the past, present, and future between them, the love she'd buried was as deep as it always was. He was in great form. Tall, harsh looking in a good way. The only tell-tale of his age was the recent silver sprinkled through the black hair. She could bet it was from her.

How she wished she take it all back. Take away his heartache and be buried in the safety of his arms.

She should finish this once and for all. She needed him out of her system so she could leave without looking back.

For his safety and Eric's.

Out of the corner of her eye, she surveyed the possibilities. She reflected back to where the men were patrolling at this time and if they were patrolling close by, she didn't have a chance. If he'd given orders for them to stay clear of the barn, she was safe.

Executing her plan, she turned and walked away.

"I'm glad you chose that route. It's going to make this so much easier."

So . . . am . . . I. God help me. So am I.

At least the men wouldn't hear her call out his name, begging for more. And that was what she knew what would happen. He definitely had a killer touch. His hands. His mouth. His whole body lethal in every way to her soul.

Without looking back, she knew he was behind her. He would hate himself for giving in, for wanting a woman who went willingly into the arms of the family he wanted executed.

Drake's steps were slow and determined.

She knew what he had wanted and he had no problems waiting for the right time in capturing it. This cat and mouse game they played back and forth would soon end. After this she had no doubt he planned to keep her in his bed for the remainder of their time. There was no way out.

For either of them.

Selena continued, unhurried in her movements. She neared the last stall. Fresh straw piled high and thick, several horse blankets draped the bottom half of the split door. She stopped. Bending over she unzipped the first ankle boot and flung it over her shoulder, then proceeded to do the same with the other one. Taking the plunge forward, she unbuttoned the first button to her jeans, then the second. Drawing the worn blue jean material over her hips, she hesitated long enough to drop them and walk away, leaving only a long cotton shirt that came to her thighs and left little to the imagination.

She slipped her hand under the shirt and pulled at the ribbon, untying one side of the scanty material. Her hand held the ribbons while the other hand caressed the inside of her leg, moving to the outer thigh. She slowly pulled the last of the ribbon, holding it.

She latched onto his gaze and let go. The silk fell between her legs.

He let out a low whistle.

She reached for a blanket to shield her body from him. He pulled her into his arms, crushing her close so she could feel what she had done to him. Her body not only knew, it rubbed against him in answer.

Her hand slipped between their bodies and found the spot she desired. Cradling. Stroking. His arms tightened. His breath coming out in short rasps against her neck. The tips of her fingers stroked him harder. Her heart beat wildly. She wanted him now more than ever, but knew she had to stop or she might forget what she had to do.

"One more taste," she whispered. She stood on her tiptoes. Her lips instinctively found his, exploring them with such hunger. She regretted the impulse, because she knew she was in danger of succumbing to their desires which would jeopardize everything she'd been planning.

She stopped the kiss cold and pushed him away. Her breath came out in small gasps. "I can't do this," she whispered, her voice jagged with emotion.

He stalled her. "You want me."

"Don't you see," she begged, placing her hand on his chest. "One of us will come out of this with scars."

Or dead, the unspoken words hung between them.

He answered her.

He held the back of her head, crushing her mouth with a kiss that rocked her to her toes. The kiss coaxed, demanded she give in to him. He devoured her lips over and over. She gasped for air, giving him the opportunity to slide in. To conquer. Large waves of desire swept through her, her legs lost all willpower, buckling from beneath her.

He caught her around the waist, refusing to let her up for air. Over and over again he tasted. Her nipples tightened at the impact. Using his legs and upper body strength, he held onto her. His labored breathing matched hers. His hand followed the hem of her shirt, slipped under to lift it over her head. The material refused to cooperate.

He tossed the shirt aside. He paused. She moaned, whispering for him to continue. He slipped his fingers in and out with slow, methodical planning. Soft mewing cries escaped her lips. He caught her when her legs buckled, threatening to let her fall.

His fingers changed the urgency in its seeking, thrusting harder and longer, deeper inside, pulling it out swiftly over and over until the wanting created an ache that was uncontrollable. The sounds were no longer soft. She wanted him to stop the aching. Her body thrashed from side to side as the aching took control, her cries grew louder. His hand silenced her cries.

"Shh . . ." he warned softly in her ear, his hand still caressing and exploring without the slightest bit of let up.

"I can't," she panted when he released her mouth. "Please, I want you," she begged, trying to pull his hand away and draw him near. Her hands fumbled at his T-shirt, needing to feel him close.

He grabbed her hands and held them. "Not yet." He kissed her swiftly on the mouth.

"Then let me go," she whispered into his mouth.

"I can't do that either, sweetheart. You're like a drug with a permanent addiction. Seeing you like a wildcat makes me want to go on forever." He cupped her bottom close to him.

She wriggled closer to feel him. She could still feel the heat through his clothing. And the hardness waiting for her.

She twisted frantically back and forth. "I'll do anything for you to end this," she promised him recklessly.

A sad smile appeared for a brief moment. "Don't make promises we both know you won't be able to keep, Selena."

"I—"

He cut her off, covering her body and her mouth with his as he lowered her to the hay. Wrapping her into his arms, he ground his hips into hers, kissing her into silence.

She breathed the words into his mouth as his tongue slid into her mouth, his body tensing at the impact of her words. It had been a long time since she'd ever breathed those words. She placed her hands on the back of his head and deepened the kiss, forcing him to slow down, to savor every living, breathing moment they had together with the ugliness shut outside.

A few unsavory words echoed in her mind, reminding her that if they went through with this beautiful moment, both might very well end up dead, because if she was any good at reading this man, his mind would no longer be alert and focused on his mission. She couldn't bear the thought of stopping him any more than she could stop her plans. It would better to leave him furious, fighting for what he wanted in order to keep him alive.

Her tongue caressed his once more and drifted away.

She lifted his head with her hands and took in every nuance, every last bit of love she could get. He needed fulfillment, especially when she'd teased him all those months before the ceremony. Two days of growth and dark locks of black raven hair with hints of silver in his crew style made it difficult to stop touching this sexy, dangerous man.

He wanted her in the worst way. Knowing instinctively she wanted him on the bottom, he allowed her to maneuver him. She straddled him, soaking in the feel of his hardness, wanting him inside.

She whispered in his ear.

He raised his arms above his head and closed his eyes. She lifted his shirt over his head. Next came his jeans. Still he kept his eyes closed, knowing she wouldn't leave him. She was too far gone herself.

Moving up and away from him, she stood staring down at him, a mixture of hope and despair written on her face. If he'd opened his eyes, he would realize her plan, making it too late for either of them. She couldn't resist sitting down one more time. With extreme care, she stretched her body over his and hugged him.

He made her ache for his touch.

Her arms moved over his, entwining her fingers with his. She gently kissed his mouth, trailing her way to his neck, nibbling on his ear. "Give me a few seconds. I want to give you something that we both will desperately need to have in order to carry on afterwards."

"Now," he ordered impatiently, opening his eyes.

"You must keep your eyes closed to feel the full impact of what I'm about to do. A few seconds won't matter, will it?"

"A few seconds. No more," his answer came out clipped and hungry, closing his eyes.

"I hope . . ." she started to whisper, but shook her head and knew she had to do this.

With great care, she picked up his clothes in one swoop, placed them in front her, and ran like hell out the door.

Chapter Twenty-Two

The warm water cascading over her helped assuage the helplessness rocking her world. Her husband wouldn't let her slide by this time. She had only delayed the inevitable, hoping for his sense of fight to kick in. He had been biting at the bit wanting answers. She scooped up water with both hands, letting it fall over the parts of her not under water. It wasn't easy controlling her sexuality, especially when it came to a single touch from Drake. Just the thought alone brought a rush of another kind of heat, a fire raging inside. Every caress and tease made it more difficult leaving him behind.

If he was still there, he would be a long way from being calm.

Drake didn't have a shy bone when it came to his body. The only part about walking back to the house naked that might tick him off was the fact he still had a hard on.

"You're not going back."

The words chilled the air. Still she didn't open her eyes.

"I have to."

"Look around you. We're in an undisclosed place. Two teams have been called here. Your Donovan won't get near you."

She opened her eyes to a determined, and naked, Drake. She avoided looking directly at him. She didn't want to renew any fires right now. She needed a plan out of here and if she wasn't focused, any opportunity in escaping would be lost.

He moved behind. His hands played with her hair, gently pulling and twisting. She sat forward as she felt him slid into the water. She leaned against his chest and sighed and wished this didn't have to end.

"You don't realize what's involved. The longer I stay here, the harder it'll be on me," she said.

She was finding it hard to ignore the slow burn quickly climaxing into a blaze which would override any common sense in this mission. The mission came first. A child came first. Drake would've made her his first priority and had a way of taking the people he loved, putting their safety first. If she would've allowed him to do it.

"Yes, I do. You owe me answers."

"Do they really matter now?" she asked.

"More now than before. The way your body reacts to my touch tells me there's more. I've seen the revulsion when Donovan touches you. Your eyes light up when you're holding Donovan's kid."

She pulled away from the comfort he provided and would've stood up, but he pulled her back into his arms.

"I would've given you a child to hold."

She climbed out the tub and walked away. She didn't want to hear his pain. It only reminded her of a life she had missed because of her private mission. She knew she had hurt him badly, but how could she have told him their marriage was put on hold? Eric wasn't his responsibility. If she'd brought him into this mess, she couldn't bear having his death on her hands.

"I know," she told him.

"We're not finished, Selena. Whatever's going on, let me in," he said.

"Oh? Like you let me in on your involvement with the Agency?"

He backed her against the sink and lifted her onto the counter, placing his legs on either side, preventing escape. His fingers trailed the inside of her thighs.

"Listen, you little cat. You don't realize what you're up against. And speaking of the Agency, you have your own little secrets. Which, by the way, explain how those beautiful legs of yours put me on the ground." He moved his hand to her breast, smiling at the reaction he received. "How much do you know about Donovan's business?"

"Enough for what I need."

"I should've hunted you down when you left me without answers. I didn't. I gave you time in case it was the cold jitters. I should've taken you at the stakeout, and then you wouldn't have been placed in this situation. You'd be home safe in my arms."

"I can handle myself."

That pissed him off. "Listen, lady. The Donovans don't give a damn about anyone but the Donovans. Especially Andrew. Do you know what he does to anyone he thinks screws him over? Or his woman? I found my kid brother dumped in a hole in the landfill area as if he were a piece of garbage. Someone had severed his anatomy off. I can't believe you couldn't have come to me for help."

She closed her eyes as if to keep him at a distance.

"Ahh, so that's how it is. I should've known. A lady who can take care of herself and doesn't need anyone else in the picture. Apparently," he said. "You needed me for something or you wouldn't have married me."

"Back off. I didn't ask you to come after me. Last time I checked my resume, the Agency was already on it before I jumped back in."

He held her in place. "Dammit," he roared. "Whatever is causing you to be reckless isn't worth it."

His worry was almost her undoing, but she had to shake it off. She slid from his reach. Her nephew wasn't an adult and needed her. No matter what it cost her.

"What is worth taking your life? Don't bother walking away, you're staying right here," he told her when she sidestepped him.

"Believe me when I say don't try to stop me," she said, unable to control the trembling in her voice. "I wish I could, but you wouldn't believe me. And you work on cold, hard facts."

"Okay, honey, here are the cold, hard facts, besides I'm horny as hell," he bit out, a low, animalistic growl following his words. "We are married and you walked out without a why or where. In fact, you ran out the back door after the ceremony. No note. No phone call. My fist connected with the bearer of the bad news. The second time he ducked and I decked the guy behind him."

Selena turned, smiling at the mortification evident in Drake's voice. "Out of curiosity, who was on the receiving end when the guy ducked?"

"You don't want to know."

Now she really wanted an answer. "Who?"

"Reverend McKinley."

She started laughing, imagining Drake's horror. She shouldn't, but she couldn't stop herself.

She sobered after a moment his stance had changed. "Don't do it, Drake. You need a clear head and so do I."

"I'm past thinking it, honey. Way past."

He picked her up.

She struggled to be released. "You've got to—"

He silenced her with a kiss.

He carried her to bed and lowered her body down.

Drake turned and fell onto the bed, taking her with him. He flipped her over. In one fluid movement, he was on top. The moment his mouth whispered into her ear, she began panting. She twisted to get away. He ignored her.

His tongue traced her ear, drawing the tip of her earlobe into his mouth. She bucked and pushed to stop the wanting. She could feel the wetness run down her legs as her body clenched and spasmed, the pain unbearable.

He held her wrists above her head.

She was trembling from the onslaught of his hands and mouth. "Drake, please," she begged. "I want you now, but we need to stop. Please be the strong one and walk away for now. I'll promise you anything."

"Not this time."

She rolled over, surprised he hadn't stopped her. Then she knew why.

The onslaught of his mouth showed no favoritism. Every part of her body felt the attack. The second his tongue switched to her breast, her body had a will of its own. Her legs had already spread for his touch.

"I love you," she whispered before she could think about its consequences.

Drake paused. "Do you think I'd be with you if you didn't?"

The determination to have her was strong in his gaze. Behind it was something she'd almost forgotten existed. Love.

"Drake, I'm sorry for the way I've handled this."

"But?"

"There's no other way. If you still want me when this is over—"

He positioned his body. "I want you now. There is another way. You're just too damned stubborn to let anyone work beside you."

She drew in a breath, feeling the heat at the hardness touching her. In an effort to calm herself and distract him, she ran her fingers over his chest, touching and smoothing the curls on it.

He stopped her.

"It won't work. Normally, I'd let you twist me around your pretty fingers, but we need this time together. I need you. Now let me love you the way a husband should love his wife in this screwed up mess around us."

She wanted that more than anything at this moment. Maybe he was right. Maybe he could help her.

"Drake?" she said. He waited, but the look told her not for long. "I—"

A knock on the door interrupted her.

He didn't look at the door but at her. They weren't done by a long shot. "Go away," he ordered.

"I told you the same thing and did you listen to me?" she whispered, teasingly.

He smiled back, forgetting where they were. "It's different and you know it."

The knocking continued.

"What?" he barked out.

Someone sighed on the other side of the door. "Drake, I know what I told you to do at the stakeout, but now isn't the time. A change of plans. He's setting up a meeting between the families. The helicopter just arrived with fresh supplies."

"Give me a minute."

"Thank you," she told him, scooting towards the head of the bed.

He stalled her. "For what?"

"Stopping."

He shook his head. "I'm not."

"But you said …"

"A minute is all I need," he said, giving no room for escape as he positioned above her. "Because when this is over, you're not leaving my arms or my bed."

With one thrust he was inside, covering her cries with his mouth.

But before she could reach orgasm, he pulled out

"Why?"

"Why?" he echoed. "Why didn't I finish what I started?"

She nodded. Too hot and too horny to stop her body from seeking him back inside.

He leaned close and placed a gentle kiss on her lips. "You were tight, wet, and hot. When I was inside, I felt the explosion in your body. You don't want anyone but me or you'd have let Donovan inside you."

"You didn't come."

"Well, right now I'm not thinking straight. All these months I've waited to be inside of you and let go, sucking every emotion, every touch, every bit of love you were willing to give. Now all I want is to have some sort of satisfaction. There's some sort of perverse pleasure knowing you can't have what you want. You're right. Now isn't the time. You obviously don't trust me enough to be in your life right now." She started to speak but he shook his head. "I won't let you go back. For any reason. Your safety is my first priority."

"What about the mission?" she said, hoping to appeal to his ethics of the Agency.

"Screw the mission. I never would've gone back to the Agency if you hadn't left me. When you did ... I felt I had nothing to live for, but seeing you mixed up with the Donovans scared some sense into me."

"You need to listen to me," she said, desperate to explain the situation and Eric.

"Later."

Two minutes later he was dressed and out the door without looking back.

She forced herself to think only of Eric, taking every ounce of sheer willpower to get dressed without chasing after Drake. She opened the drapes. The skies had darkened to a grey outcast. With nighttime almost upon them, she had a better chance of getting out of here undetected.

Well, at least long enough to get a head start.

Soft scratching noises alerted her she wasn't alone. Half expecting the door to open, she moved out of the direct line of vision and turned off the light. She eyed the gap under the door. Someone was there. She could see light except one area.

She opened the door and stepped out, screaming Drake's name when she saw who it was. A foul-smelling cloth covered her mouth and nose.

She passed out.

*

Drake heard Selena call out his name. Something was wrong. He raced up the stairs.

"It's okay. She fainted. I was able to catch her before she hit the floor."

Drake stared hard as Jeremy carried Selena over to the bed. "What the hell are you doing here?"

Jeremy set her gently down. "I had a message you wanted to see me about a leak."

"You heard wrong. I can take care of any leaks in this house. When did you get in?"

"This morning."

"I see." Drake didn't trust him. Not only did this snot nose kid get this job without earning it, he was butting into his men and his mission. Now he was in his wife's room. "I'll meet you downstairs. I'll take it from here."

Jeremy looked at her and then at Drake. "She's a beautiful woman."

Drake didn't take the bait. "Yes, but she's with Donovan."

As Jeremy left the room, he told Drake, "I hope you don't forget that. Being taken in by a beautiful woman can be dangerous to your health."

Yours maybe, Drake thought. He quickly felt for Selena's pulse. When he found one, he went to the door to see if the hall was clear. He had to get her out of here. His gut told him she wasn't safe. He started to pick her up but Barry's voice on his ear piece forced him to postpone moving her.

"You really need to hear this. Andrew's talking about Selena."

Drake checked the hall again. Jeremy had vanished. "Where's Jeremy?"

"Outside talking to the men."

Drake listened. He didn't know whether to hug Selena or kick her butt for not telling him.

"Meet me in your room," he told Barry.

*

Jeremy gave it another few minutes before he went back into Selena's room. His father, Danten, was head of the Agency and had pulled a lot of strings in getting him this job. His father's private business with Andrew was taking these risks—but did his father take the risks anymore? No, it was Jeremy who had to.

He scowled. They didn't pay him enough to deal with this bullshit.

It didn't take long to get to the launch pad and it wouldn't take long for Drake to realize he had taken Selena. His cover was blown. He was no longer an asset to his father or Andrew.

If he hadn't grabbed Selena when he had, Andrew would've had him killed and buried him like Drake's brother.

The helicopter pilot was waiting to take off. Jeremy handed Selena over to one of Andrew's men.

"Hold it right there!" Drake yelled.

Jeremy glanced over his shoulder and saw Drake aiming his sidearm.

"You're too late." Jeremy climbed in the helicopter.

The co-pilot aimed artillery at Selena.

Drake let a few expletives out and leaped towards the helicopter as it lifted.

A shot rang out and Jeremy jerked back, taking Drake with him. They landed on the ground.

*

Drake shoved the kid off of him, disgusted at the number of betrayals running deep in their team. The helicopter was too high up to try again. He glanced at Jeremy, wanting to beat the hell out of the kid for betraying Selena and the Agency, but if he did, he'd kill him. He checked Jeremy over, finding he had been hit in the shoulder and would make it. Jeremy wasn't going anywhere at the moment, but Drake wasn't taking any more chances and handcuffed him to the railing.

Drake called Danten. "I found our leak. He's handcuffed on the top level. He's all yours. If you don't get your kid out of my face soon, I might just have to have it out with him."

Drake saw the kid had regained consciousness and was listening to the call. The kid's arrogance drained away. Whatever was running through the kid's mind terrified him, but Jeremy wasn't his problem any longer. Drake left Jeremy for his men to watch over until Danten arrived. He had to make it to the meeting and hopefully save his wife.

And their marriage.

Chapter Twenty-Three

Jeremy knew pity when he saw it. Hadn't he pitied his own victims when he'd been ordered to abduct the women? But he knew his father and Andrew. Knew the power they welded. Their wrath was terrifying. His career was over—neither his father nor Andrew would take chances in having their cover blown.

Jeremy had one last confession. He asked the guard to call Drake.

"Drake? Tell Larry I'm sorry. He can find his daugh—"

*

A gunshot rang through.

By the time Drake and the others reached Jeremy, a bullet had been put between his eyes. The rooftop was otherwise empty, and there was no sign of whoever had killed him.

Clenched with frustration, Drake called Larry. He half-hoped voicemail would pick up. He didn't want to deal with Larry's reaction to being so close to finding out what had happened to Lacey.

"Hello, Drake," Martha answered. "I hope you realize how long it took Larry to relax."

"I'm sorry, Martha, but this couldn't wait. Is he around?"

"Right here. Spill it."

Drake hesitated. "Larry, take it off speaker phone."

"That's kind of hard to do at the moment. Martha's holding the phone hostage. I think she's afraid you're going to ruin the moment."

That was more than Drake wanted to know. "It's serious. It's about your...Martha, I'd rather you didn't hear any of this."

"Drake, don't mess with me right now. You know the chain reaction," Martha said.

Drake knew all right. If Martha wasn't happy, Larry wasn't and then neither were his men.

"Finish it," Larry bit out.

"It's about Lacey."

Silence. There was no going back now. Drake continued, "We found the leak. It was Jeremy. I left him on the rooftop, handcuffed, waiting for his father. He admitted he knew where Lacey is being held."

"What do you mean *knew?*" White asked.

"There's another leak. By the time we got up to the rooftop, Jeremy was taken out."

Drake didn't like being the bearer of this news. Martha was crying in the background and Larry wasn't saying a word.

"I'm sorry, Martha. I wish we'd gotten to Jeremy in time."

"At least she's still alive. I want my baby home, Larry," Martha said quietly and began sobbing again.

Drake didn't know which was worse, finding your daughter dead or abducted into the human trafficking world, hidden.

"I want to be kept informed. Of everything," Larry said quietly.

"One last thing. They have Selena."

*

Selena woke to dampness seeping into her, causing her bones and muscles to ache with such intensity she wanted to weep, but she couldn't. She felt as if every ounce of fluid had been sucked dry, her tongue swollen. She couldn't tell how long she'd been lying here. Her eyes felt gritty and her body was starting to shake. The closed-in feelings weren't far behind.

She was tied up, her arms and legs bound tightly, already cramping. The only light came from under the crack across the room. A shadow moved and blocked the light before moving away.

If she didn't get out of here, Drake and Eric were going to die. She should have trusted Drake to help her from the beginning. She should have told him everything.

An explosion went off in the next room. Wood splintered. She rolled as far as she could until she butted against a barrier.

The door creaked.

Knowing her luck, it was probably the black knight instead of her white knight rescuing her. Heavy footsteps clunked against the wood.

"Do you need a hand?"

The godfather, Nick. The man she'd come to dub the black knight.

"Why do I always get the comedians?" Selena asked.

Nick rolled her over, none too gently, and with a quick jerk she was freed. She sat up and rubbed her wrists. A slight movement from the corner of her eye told her he'd used a knife to cut her loose.

"I can always put them back on," he suggested, dryly.

"You're definitely funny." Getting to her feet, she left him behind. But not for long.

"How do you propose to get there?" he asked.

"With your car, of course."

"You take a lot for granted." He headed her way.

She sighed. "You think I don't know that. I took too much for granted and might have lost the best man in my life. Why are you helping me?"

"You remind me of someone," he started to say, holding the door open.

"That's a good pickup line." She waited in the alley for him.

"It's not a pickup line. It's true." Dressed in black, he blended well with the night. "You do remind me of someone. Someone I owe a great deal. It's a little late, but I think she'd understand."

"Of course, rescuing a lady in distress wasn't out of the goodness of your heart," she murmured.

She didn't have to have light to see the mocking glint in his eye. "Keep it up, sweetheart, and you'll be thumbing your way back. Do you treat Drake like this?"

Selena took a quick take of her surroundings and the bike to her left. Deciding this was his mode of transportation she swung her leg over and patted the seat in front of her. "No. You're lucky, I'm saving the best for Drake."

"My sympathies are with him."

She grinned. "Tell him in the morning. I need to ask a favor."

"They all say that, but do they know the price tag?"

"Drake will kill you if you even suggest touching this body."

*

When they arrived, they found the Donovan house deserted. Not one gunman skulked around the corner. Even Eric and Mary were gone. Selena grabbed her sister's diary and shoved it in her bag and quickly changed into all-black clothing. She ran into Andrew's office. On his desk was a note. She read it and stuffed it in her pocket.

She jumped into the back of the waiting limo. "They're at the warehouse."

"Is that why you took so long? I could've told you that." Her black knight signaled to his driver.

They rode in silence, each deep in their own thoughts.

Selena pointed to the phone. "Do you mind?"

He consented with a nod. "Would it matter if I did?"

She punched in the number, praying it was still the same number, knowing without a doubt her black knight would keep it in his little black book. She held the speaker button until a voice echoed in the back.

"Selena?"

"I love you."

The black knight took the phone. "Drake, she's fine. I'll take good care of her. Yes, I know you'll kick my ass, or anyone else's, if she's touched or harmed in any way. She's a little too wild for my taste. She's very headstrong. You have my condolences. By the way, she's determined to go to the warehouse. Yes? Are you sure? Because I will deliver the message in the manner in which my mood takes me." The black knight hung up and gestured they had arrived at their destination.

"Honey, close your eyes."

She eyed him suspiciously.

"Just do it." She did against her better judgment. "Drake said to tell you this ... You better not die because this is a prelude to forever ..." The black knight pulled her into his arms and kissed her deeply.

After he let her go, she saw the anguish written all over him. "Who was she?"

He caressed her swollen lips and didn't answer. "I will come to you later. Don't worry," he said, grinning at the suspicion written all over her before she stepped out of the limo. "Drake would hunt me down."

Selena winked as she pulled the gun from her boot. She ran low and fast, fading into the shadows. She looked over her shoulder. Her black knight had gone.

She'd been alone far too long, worrying who could be trusted and who couldn't in the games of good versus evil. The two men she knew she could count on were her husband and her nephew. Her sister had written everything in her diary. Everything except naming Eric's father. Somehow, she didn't think it was Andrew.

She crouched behind crates.

Andrew had called all the families together, stating it was time to make peace. He had insisted the power was in sharing territories and allegiance, banding together for a higher power. It would be interesting to see who believed Andrew.

The sound of machinery cut through the silent night.

This wasn't right. No one was allowed outside. No backup. No guns. Rules, even silent ones, were to be obeyed as a gesture of courtesy. This was definitely a sign of trouble.

Two cranes, with huge wrecking balls attached, rolled by. They split up. One parked at the end and the other around the corner, out of sight. She glanced at the crane nearest her. A construction hat hid the driver's eyes as he lit a cigarette, one foot propped on the steering wheel. He hunkered down with the hat over his face as if to give the impression he was taking a break.

She scanned the area.

Crates were situated around the docks. A bulldozer sat in the middle of the lot. She could barely make out the yellow hat in the cab. Thick black wires wove among the boxes and machinery. She spotted the men crouched in the darkened corners of the dock.

Something flew past her.

She flattened against the warehouse and looked up when she realized it was a lit cigarette. They knew she was here. Not only was Andrew setting up his competition, but her as well. He needed his pawns in place before checkmate.

She only needed two pawns. Surprise and Drake.

*

Drake was tired of the games. He wanted his wife in his arms and out of Andrew's way.

"You're not focused."

"Getting my wife out safely and killing Andrew is not being focused? I'd say I'm pretty damn focused. Wait. Kill."

Barry got in his face. "You've lost the main picture. All the families are here for a reason. The docks are wired with explosives. Someone has maneuvered machinery and crates at all the exits but one. Why the old man wants this so bad, I don't know. There's a hidden agenda somewhere." Barry hauled Drake against the metal.

"If you get your head out of your ass, maybe you can save your wife and the mission." Barry let go. "I'm your partner and friend, not some pansy you can push around because you're hurting and pissed off. You've reached the quota on that one."

Drake chuckled.

"Now he's laughing at me," Barry groaned. "I get no respect around here."

"I'm not laughing at you. I'm just surprised it took you this long to give it back."

"Playing nursemaid is not my style."

Barry wasn't nursemaid poster material. Nursemaids didn't carry knives or machine guns. They definitely weren't angelic. He hadn't seen Barry nurture anyone except his guns. Even the women he took out weren't exposed to a softer Barry. They were treated with kindness and respect, but Barry wasn't the bleeding heart with anyone.

Barry growled. "Quit smilin'. I'm taking a vacation when this is all over."

"That's what I said right before I met Selena and fell in love." Drake held up his hand. "They're coming out. That includes Selena, Andrew's son, and the old man."

Barry grabbed the binoculars offered and handed them to Drake.

Twenty-foot high barbed wire fencing enclosed the warehouse district. The general public viewed it as keeping intruders out of the warehouses. Though the warehouses seemed empty most of the time, rumor had it one of the opposing families had sent someone to scout around. By the time the man had reached the other side, his hands had been shredded, and as he'd dropped to the ground, his body convulsed. He'd tried climbing back over the fence when five dogs pulled him to the ground. The next morning his body had been found under a bridge. The autopsy found poison in his blood stream. Apparently, the barbed wire had been coated with a fast-acting poison.

Drake saw Selena being led out of the warehouse by Andrew's men, depositing her next to Andrew. Selena reached for Eric, but Eric was handed to the housekeeper. Old man Donovan was silent and rigid, the rage barely below surface. Andrew was smiling and laughing with everyone, playing the perfect host, shaking hands, patting their backs.

Andrew stopped and looked towards their way and drew Selena close.

"Easy. You can rip him to shreds soon enough," Barry said, holding Drake back when Andrew gave a mocking salute as if to say he knew Drake was nearby.

"There's no way the kid had time to alert Andrew we're on to him." Drake's hands tightened around the binoculars. "There's another leak."

*

"You're hurting me," Selena said through clenched teeth.

Andrew dug his fingers into her arm. "Smile and look pretty. Hopefully, you have more brains than your sister. You could've had it all."

"No. Wasn't my sister's heart enough?" she asked, discontinuing the charade. "She loved you so much she forgot she had a family."

"Love isn't all it's cracked up to be." He gave a salute over the crowd. "Enough. It's time to get down to why we're here."

"Melding the families together for unity?"

He whispered, "Honey, when has a Donovan ever shared power? I'm feeling generous. Since you still hold a place in my heart for saving my son, you're free to leave."

He shook his head as she reached for Eric again. "He stays with me."

She wasn't into begging, but her nephew's life was different. "Isn't there anything that can change your mind?"

"No. I had to learn at a young age what was expected of a

Donovan. He will, too."

She couldn't leave him in the midst of all this.

Andrew made a motion.

Selena felt the hard metal against her back. She looked back at Pitter Patter Man. He was enjoying this too much. Pitter Patter jabbed her hard and jerked his head to the rear of the building.

He shoved her. "Go. Or I'll shoot against the boss' orders."

She walked.

At the gate, the metal door slid open and a limo pulled up in front of her. The back door opened. A hand waved her in. She wasn't sure whose side it was on and wasn't about to find out.

A familiar voice beckoned her in. "Drake promised he'd kick my ass if anything happened to you."

Selena leaned in. "You seem to be my shadow these days. What gives?"

"Just get in. You're not safe."

"Stop," a voice called out.

Selena turned.

Mary came out from behind the stacked crates. She held a large, soft woven basket by the handles. Mary approached the limo, her face shielded by a black shawl draped over her. "You forgot this." She held it out.

Selena stared at the basket.

A noise came from within.

She met Mary's eyes with understanding. "It does look familiar. May I look at it?"

Mary lifted the basket towards her, then drew it back close to her chest, holding tight. She pulled the handles apart. As if checking out the contents and seeing all was intact, a wistful smile appeared on her face. When she looked at Selena, there were tears in her eyes. She held it out to Selena.

Selena's hand grazed Mary's trembling one. Whatever connection Eric and Mary held, she would make sure it never ended and relayed this to Mary as only one woman could to another.

Mary nodded, letting Selena take it from her, and walked away.

Selena had to ask, "Why?"

Mary signed, "The time has come for me to take care of personal business. I made a promise to someone a long time ago."

Once inside the limo, Selena lifted the blanketed bundle from within the basket. She pushed the ends aside and gazed upon her sleeping nephew with love. "Everyone is bent on fulfilling promises lately."

"What about you?"

"No."

"Didn't you make silent promises to the man you love?"

"I failed Theresa by not being there when she needed me most. I allowed my job to interfere with family needs."

"Just like your marriage."

"That's not fair," she said.

"Do you think you're being fair? I should've taken the woman I loved far away, but I let my job interfere. I didn't trust her love enough to see us through it all. Now she's gone."

"I'm sorry."

"It's not me you have to tell." To his driver, "You know where."

Eric began crying.

Selena patted his cheek, soothingly. "It's okay, little one. Auntie Selena will have you home soon."

Eric cried louder. She searched the bag for extra diapers.

"Give him to me while you do that," he said.

She handed him over and checked the bag.

"Stop the car!" The car pulled over. "Get out now," he ordered her.

"I'm not leaving Eric again." She glared at him, refusing to budge.

"If you don't get out, you're going to die."

She tried to take Eric from his arms, but he pulled Eric away. "I thought you were on our side."

"I'm on no one's side. Haven't you figured that out yet? I'm not trying to keep you from Eric. Andrew wired Eric."

Eric screamed at the top of his lungs.

"Do you think Mary knew?"

He shrugged. When Selena leapt out of the limo, he followed with Eric. He laid Eric on the edge of the seat and undid the tabs of his disposable diaper. Selena watched in horror as the man she'd dubbed black knight studied the explosive device secured on Eric's body.

She reached to undo it.

"Don't touch it. We don't know if that will set it off. Now run!"

"I'm not going to let him die alone."

Someone grabbed her arm and yanked her out of the car. In desperation, she struggled to get back to Eric. The driver was stronger and determined to follow his boss' orders. He dragged her away.

Eric screamed louder.

Selena refused to watch from safety while her nephew was about to be blown to pieces. She rounded on the driver and punched his Adam's apple. The driver held tight even as he gasped for breath. She kicked him in the groin. The second he let go she raced for the car door, wrenching it from the Black Knight's hands as he was closed it. She checked to make sure the keys were still in the ignition and locked the doors.

"I'm not leaving. Wherever he goes, I go. Even if it means death."

*

Drake watched Selena being led from front stage. Andrew wasn't the generous type. In fact, he wouldn't put it past Andrew to waste her in one of his experiments. "Have we heard anything from our informant?"

"No," Cam said.

Drake's main objective was to complete his mission and save his wife. The best chance of succeeding was using Cam, their best long-range shooter. He could take a walnut out of a squirrel's paws without touching a hair on it.

"Can you take out Andrew?" he asked.

"I can take them both out." He meant Selena, too.

"I didn't ask that," Drake said. He fought the rising anger, knowing they would question his loyalty otherwise. Barry was the only member of his team who knew everything. Drake didn't trust anyone when it came to Selena.

"Yes."

"Take him out. Now," Drake ordered.

Cam aimed, his finger squeezed gently on the trigger. He repositioned the butt against his shoulder and looked through the scope again before releasing the trigger. "It's too late."

Drake checked it out for himself.

"Don't trust me after all these years? Should I have myself reassigned to another team?"

"Whatever you need to do—Do it." Drake felt his phone vibrate and answered it. After he hung up, he announced, "The place is rigged to blow."

Barry came up beside him. "Our informant?"

Drake nodded, taking the binoculars and scoping out the area for Selena. She was nowhere around. "Where did Selena go?"

"The back. On top of the bombings, someone's finally made their move on Andrew's son. They went over the edge and wired Andrew's son with a new type of explosive," Barry passed on the info as he received it.

"Which direction did they take his son?" His gut crawled with fear.

"To the back. Hey, where are you going?" Barry asked.

There were two things Drake knew in life—he wasn't losing to Selena to Andrew and he was going to hide her away before he turned completely grey.

He hadn't gotten more than halfway around the warehouse when the explosion went off.

*

At the sound of the explosion, the families sprang into action, shouting orders. Andrew's men pointed automatic weapons at them, refusing to allow them to leave.

The consigliore shouted at Andrew, "What is this? You want it to end in this way?"

"You do not care you have dishonored the family?" another asked.

"As a matter of fact, I do," Andrew said. "Wouldn't you?" He was his own family. The men under him were just out for whatever they could get, and in his book, that wasn't family. He didn't give a damn about honor or family. There wasn't honor in this family. He definitely didn't give a damn about the code among the families.

Andrew wanted revenge.

One consigliore from the west end spoke softly, "Gentlemen," he included the other consigliores as he addressed Andrew. "I was not sure what to expect from our newest family member. So ... I brought a gift he could not refuse."

*

"Are you sure you want it this way?"

Selena listened to Eric's jabbering on the baby monitor. It would be awhile before he fell asleep. He needed stability considering what he had experienced.

"I don't have any other alternative," she said.

There was a pause which would surely be followed by a lecture or caustic commentary knowing him.

"Everyone has other avenues they can take. Call him," Nick said.

Nick was beginning to be a pain. And right.

"You know I'm right, Selena."

"But that doesn't make it any easier."

"If you don't — "

She had a right to her privacy and she could take care of Eric and herself just fine. "What are you going to do? Kick us out of the cabin?"

Nick sighed. "No. I have my reasons for taking you there. It's yours for as long as you'd like. Just remember this … I will collect what you owe. The place has been stocked and the delivery guy won't be back for a month." He sighed again. "Keep low, will you? It's not over yet."

"I will." She thought she heard him mutter, *You will, my ass.*

She laughed. "Eric's life is important to me and I won't put him in jeopardy."

"If Drake finds you, I can't help you."

No one could. Drake had to have been told she had died when the car blew up. He would stop looking for her. "It's over. As far as anyone thinks, Eric and I are cremated. Life goes on and so will we," she said.

Eric's babbling had stopped. She walked to his room and peeked in. Sleeping. "Somehow a thank you is not enough for what you've done."

"All you need to do is stay out of trouble." Softly, the black knight added, "Take care of Eric."

Chapter Twenty-Four

Selena filled up the bathtub, forcing herself to get a grip. She was no good to anyone if she wasn't staying calm.

Too many deaths and too many betrayals on everyone's part, including her own. She should've trusted Drake from the start, but how could she have known? He hadn't told her about his involvement with the Agency any more than she'd told him about hers.

She loved Drake with all her heart. It had taken his hard edge to pierce her concrete wall. She wanted Eric and Drake safe, but getting Eric and Drake in the same room without Andrew's men waiting to take them out was almost impossible. Heaven knew she wanted to turn to his touch. To feel the warmth and security he provided in those arms. She wished now he would've finished making love to her at the safe house.

Dropping her clothes to the floor, she stepped into the water, its warmth soothing. Longing seeped into her heart and body.

She needed Drake.

A shadow crossed the light.

She stilled her mind, quickly slipping into her clothes. Nothing sited in her peripheral vision, but she wasn't taking any chances.

Someone was in the house.

She ran to Eric's room. Eric was on his stomach, sucking his thumb. Still out like a light. She checked the bedroom and kitchen. All clear. Her feet were silent on the cool wooden floor. A fire had been started in the fireplace some time ago. The flames were high and the pieces of wood half licked.

Someone was playing with her.

A scuffling noise came from behind.

She turned. Movement came from the hallway.

Eric.

She retrieved her gun from the purse and headed down the hall. The only exit was through her. Someone grabbed her from behind, wrenching the gun from her hand. She fought to turn, but the man held her tightly against him. He was stronger than her, stilling her movements.

She twisted her body and laced her foot around his leg. Her hand reached behind her and went into claw formation. She brought her head forward. His hand pulled her head back and held her chin firmly. It was then she smelled the familiarity of the past catching up with her.

Drake.

"I warned you." He turned her around and kissed her thoroughly, one hand held her head, the other, showing her what she was about to receive.

She fought the rising emotions of needing him inside. She had to stay focused.

His tongue seduced as he kissed her again. She brought her knee between his legs. He tensed, but when she stroked him with her knee, he relaxed. A hand curved around her bottom and stilled.

He groaned. She wasn't wearing anything beneath it. He lifted the shirt and caressed.

Time had run out.

"Drake."

"Larry was right. That killer smile of yours is hazardous to your health. He told me how you charmed and blackmailed your way back into the Agency. But right now, talking isn't what I had in mind."

Heat raced through her veins. She wanted to run but couldn't. Her body and mind warred.

Drake tossed his shirt to the floor. His fingers moved to the button on his jeans. He undid the button and pulled the zipper down. He tossed boots and jeans to the side. She stared longingly at the hard-contoured chest, wanting, then shifted her gaze further below.

"Take your shirt off," he said.

"I don't think that's a good idea," she whispered.

He smiled. "You're right, but it doesn't matter at this point."

Heat pulsated, spilling down her leg. Her breath hitched. She backed away. He pushed her on the bed, kissing her while plunging two fingers inside. Her hips arched away, wanting, needing, yet fighting the heat. He held her in place. With slow, even thrusts, he continued. She bit back a scream.

"Honey, there's no need to hold back. No one can hear you and I promise, there's more to come." He moved in and out, slow, long strokes, drawing each one back, holding, waiting, until she had almost caught her breath. He removed his fingers. Positioning himself above her, he plunged inside within one hard stroke.

She thrashed back and forth. Still he refused to let her go.

With each stroke, he gave warning, "You. Will. Never. Do. This. Again."

The heat in his eyes matched the heat between her legs, the intensity rising to a peak. Even if she wanted to tell him she'd do it again if she had to, she knew better. The warning signs were all there.

Horny. Hot. Worry. And love.

She clenched her legs together, stilling the flow of heat.

He refused the power struggle.

She tightened her hold. "Why didn't you just find someone else?"

Desire and the need to touch her body overcame him as he slowly buried deeper inside with each thrust. She couldn't control him any more than she could control herself and came as Drake released, spilling inside her. She moved away, partially sitting against the headboard, coming down with each breath, each panting, placing her hand on his chest.

"I love you with every ounce of blood in my body. Move the hand, Selena. We are not finished."

She closed her eyes and took a deep breath, willing herself to not to overheat from the rising explosion. "Drake."

"Lady, you have ten seconds to spill."

"Why didn't you find someone to care of your...your...well, you know." She inched away. "Men have needs."

He placed a light kiss on her temple. "Is that so? And did you have needs taken care of?"

She knew better than to accept the gauntlet, because the casual question had a bite hidden in the midst. She hadn't slept with anyone.

"But you would have," he answered for her, reading her mind.

Drake meant Andrew. She couldn't lie to him especially now even though she would have done it to save Eric only. "Yes."

"You do realize who you're married to? You would've committed bigamy for that scum?"

"Not for him."

"It sure wasn't for us." Drake closed his eyes and sighed. He rolled away.

She didn't move.

*

Drake couldn't get past her defenses. In her state of mind, she had one purpose. Andrew's baby. For some reason she felt the need to exclude him. From her life. Her work. And her heart.

How was he going to get through to her? He'd be damned if he let her continue to put herself in jeopardy. Right now the frustration of not touching her, making up for lost time and knowing she couldn't trust him was eating away every bit of self control.

He walked away.

He had to get a grip on the situation.

The fire had nearly died out, leaving small traces of flames licking the coals. He grabbed three logs and threw them on the burning bed. Sparks flew out, but soon changed direction to cover the logs. He listened.

"Don't stop me from going after Andrew," she warned. "You

won't like me if you do."

He advanced. "I think it's you who's not going to like me." He didn't hurry. He didn't need to. She had nowhere to go but past him.

She tried.

She didn't succeed any further than into his arms.

"As long as Andrew is on the run, you're with me." He lifted her into his arms. "You have two choices. Safe with me. Willing or unwilling."

She wound her hand around his neck, caressed the hairs curling at his nape. She slid her finger down his lips and pressed a lingering kiss upon them. He slipped his tongue between her lips when she would've backed away. She sighed into the kiss.

"I love you," he said.

*

He waited until he she had fallen asleep and called Larry. "Larry."

"Speak."

Drake laughed. "Nice to hear you're among the living, too."

"Listen," Larry said, lowering his voice. "I've got three minutes exactly. Martha's walking with her friends. After you left, all hell broke loose. The families all turned on the Donovans. Even the Donovans turned on each other. More wounded than killed which means their attorneys will get them free on technicalities. It didn't go down the way you would've thought, having them cornered like cattle at the slaughterhouse. The moment the team moved in, they turned on us, uniting as a front. It's like you can insult your own brother, but someone else do it and you're in for a beating."

"What about old man Donovan?" Drake asked, listening for any sign of movement.

"He vanished. Later someone found him slumped in the corner having a heart attack."

"Andrew?" It was too quiet.

"No trace. I don't like it."

Drake didn't either. "If he's heading this way, I won't kill him. At least not until I find out where your daughter is." *Then I'll kill him.*

Larry sighed. "I'm serious. Martha can't take another dead-end lead."

The line went dead. Larry wasn't in for goodbyes.

A shadow crossed over. Selena had dressed.

"Drake?"

He reached for her as she came closer, scooping her into his arms.

"I'm sorry I kept my past a secret. I shouldn't have left you that day."

He sighed deeply. "But you would do it again, wouldn't you?"

When she didn't answer, he had his answer.

"Where do we go from here?"

"The only place you two are going is hell."

Andrew.

Drake reached for his gun.

"I wouldn't, but if you want to, who am I to stop you?" Andrew pointed the gun at Selena.

Drake stopped cold.

"After you left, my father gave everyone the news … It seems I jumped the gun on proposing. You're cemented into this family whether you like it or not. It seems you and I, dear sister, have the same father but different mothers." He waved his gun in the air for her to come to his side. "Theresa wasn't related to me. Dad had hand-picked her as my wife. He had said the marriage would bring true blood to the family." Andrew laughed, squeezing the trigger slowly. "Dad always twisted his words."

"I'm sorry, Drake."

Drake's eyes narrowed, growing blacker by the second as he watched Selena's intent. "You're a Donovan. You can never come back to me. You're as dead as he is."

"I died a long time ago, honey," she said.

Drake's voice was as cold as ice, his body filled with hatred. It was his eyes that gave his love away. Out of the corner of his eye,

Drake noticed a few shadows crossing the yard in the moonlight. A beam of light hit Selena.

Andrew noticed and seemed to welcome the higher octave of danger.

Drake dived for Andrew, taking him to the floor. Andrew's gun slid across the floor.

Selena dived for Andrew's gun, pushing the fire away from Drake. Andrew kicked her in the ribs and fired rapidly.

Andrew aimed his gun. Drake pulled the trigger. Andrew fell to the ground. Doors flew open. Glass shattered as the team entered, aiming their weapons at Andrew. Drake pulled Selena into his arms.

Danten strode into the room.

"I'll take over. Just handcuff Donovan," Danten ordered.

Several men hauled Andrew up, slamming him into the wall as they handcuffed him.

"I'll meet the boys back at HQ," Danten said. "I'll process this one myself."

Andrew smirked. Not in the least bit intimidated.

Danten shoved Andrew forward, keeping him slightly in front as they walked towards the helicopter. The co-pilot hopped out and opened the door. The pilot fell to the side, clutching his side. Shots rang out. Someone shouted for Andrew to halt. Wind whipped until the dirt in the fields looked like a cyclone. Another helicopter had been hiding. More shots rang out.

Selena, Drake and Danten made it to the pilot at the same time. Before he died, the pilot pointed to Danten.

*

The parking lot was almost empty. Larry's car and an unknown sat side by side. Drake didn't like leaving Selena alone. So he did the next best thing … he'd given orders to have guards 24/7 at her place while he sought answers.

The halls of the Agency were barren with the exception of

numbers on the doors. No names. No directory. There was more to Larry forcing him on leave. More to Larry having a cabin in the same town as Selena.

Heated voices came at full blown speed as he narrowed the distance. Two women. One was Martha.

The other—Mary.

Larry's dead silence was a giveaway as the two women let him have it.

Drake should've left him take the heat but being comrades, he just couldn't do that to another man. Two against one wasn't fair.

He opened the door.

Martha, Larry, and Mary stood in a circle. The women had their hands on their hips, their facial expressions frozen and pissed off. They rounded on Drake, daring him to side against them.

Hell had definitely frozen over.

He walked around Larry and sat in his chair, propping his feet on the desk. He'd wait until Larry was too exhausted to hide the truth. Women had this unfailing energy in heated times like this.

"Drake should have the specifics in how you arranged them to meet," Martha said. "Tell him how you purchased a cabin a week before you forced him on leave, offering him a cool down place for as long as he needed it."

Drake didn't want to watch this one unfold, but he couldn't stop himself. "I'd like to hear more on how you played matchmaker."

Larry gnawed on his words carefully before answering, "I liked the cabin. I didn't think twice buying it or offering it to a good man when he needs to get his ass straightened out."

"Don't go belligerent and almighty on me or I'll leave you with these two. Alone," Drake said, stressing the last word. "You might need me to sweep what's left of you into the recycling bin."

Larry took one look at what lay ahead of him and surrendered. "All right, but if you breathe one damn word of this to anyone, I'll—I'll sick them on you."

"Don't worry about me. It's Selena you need to worry about. Is Eric okay?" he asked, making sure he was facing Mary.

Mary turned before he'd finished and nodded. "Yes, he's fine. When you and Selena have a place to call home, Eric and I will come live with you. Between the three of us, he'll be safe," she said.

Martha wasn't taking it well—whatever had gone down earlier. Stepping back, she massaged both temples. Larry came forward only to be stalled by her foreboding expression and warning. "I have a headache. I have this sinking feeling it's going to be a very dry spell for you." To Mary. "I don't like you. Yet, I, also, have this sinking feeling we're going to be very good friends. It'll be like watching reruns of *Reba*." Hand on door. "Drake, call me. We have some planning to do."

Drake grinned at Larry as she sauntered out the door. "Way ahead of you, Martha. Actually, I think you'll like what I have in mind."

*

"I never meant to hurt Martha," Mary said.

"How could any of us know how much one family could screw with so many lives?" Larry made the decision he thought he would never make. Retirement once this was over.

Larry drew Mary into his arms, not caring what Drake thought.

He needed it and she needed it. The lost time, the heartache, and a lost child.

"I would've told you I was pregnant, but Donovan knew who you were. He promised he would leave you alone if I stayed. I had to stay. Now our son is out there," Mary said.

Larry's fingers shook as he wiped her tears away. He pulled her away and kissed her cheek.

A shadow darkened the room.

"I'll take over from here, White." A bald man stood in the doorway.

Mary spun towards the sound of his voice. A man she had left behind in order to protect whom she thought was her son.

"Who is he?" Larry asked.

"She is no longer your concern, White."

"Mack, I can handle this," Mary said, seeing the residual anger of the past in his eyes. To White, "He was there when you weren't. If he hadn't found me, I would never have survived."

Touching White's face tenderly with the palm of her hand, she looked into his eyes. He knew she was saying goodbye to the past; it had to be this way. He knew his eyes showed his own goodbye. She kissed him gently on the lips, knowing Mack wouldn't like it but would accept it. This time only.

Mary ran into Mack's waiting arms.

*

Drake watched Larry's face fall as closure settled into place. He nodded towards Martha's picture. "She's one helluva lady."

"Yes, she is." He picked up the frame. "She deserves better. I hope I can give her back the daughter she prays for every night."

"We will. I may not be here for new missions, but I can guarantee I will help finish the old ones." Larry's daughter was still alive. They would all come to his aid.

Chapter Twenty-Five

Everyone in Heaven's Way had voted against Selena's involvement in decorating for Christmas. Taking the only alternative, she leaned back into the easy chair and grumbled.

Mack patted her head.

John, Henry, and Tom hadn't stopped kissing on their wives. Though she couldn't put a finger on it, she had the impression they were glad they hadn't dated her. Just about everyone had shown up with the exception of Mrs. Irons.

Selena watched an ornament fall from the tree and roll towards her chair. Her fingers itched to pick it up, to do something other than watch, but Mack had caught the slight movement and smiled. He would tell Drake if she mutinied. There was way too much mothering here.

She caught Mary's signs from the other side of the living room.

"Time will fly," Mary signed again. Mary left the decorating to the others and came over to Selena. "Come on, let's go for a walk."

It was better than sitting here. Selena used her hands to push herself up and fell backwards. She tried several times before giving up on independence. Together they laughed as their teamwork did the trick. Selena patted her rounded stomach and accepted the shawl Drake draped around her shoulders.

Mary and Selena took the trail through the woods which sheltered them from prying eyes and the elements. Dark skies threatened to spill two more inches of snow. Drake wasn't letting her out of his sight until the baby was born and Selena couldn't help with Eric as much as she'd like due to the doctor's orders of taking it easy.

Mary held the branch back for Selena to pass under.

"You realize Drake will not let you near a mission again? Losing you a second time would kill him."

"Why did you go back to Donovan after you'd had a chance to escape that hell?"

"It was a different kind of hell. I didn't have to endure the wifely hells of all hells. Being several steps below wives, runners, and bodyguards, I didn't have many rights. But if I tended my duties, they ignored me." Mary must've seen what was coming because she addressed it next. "Donovan was the wandering type. He liked women he employed. When he'd finished with them … there's nothing like a woman scorned, especially one, our housekeeper, the real Mary, who had lost her babies to Donovan's hands. Mary found a way to inform me of my husband's plans to kill me. Wrong or right, I'd traded my son with another woman in case I didn't survive, but the exchange somehow went askew. Mack gave up his life to watch over the other child, while I stayed with Andrew. As a woman, Mary knew the importance of a child having his mother around while growing up and suggested we change places."

It had been a risky plan with little chance of success, Selena understood. But the alternative was a certain death.

"If I were dead, Donovan wouldn't be able to look for me," Mary said. "When Donovan tried to have me killed, Mack saved my life. I had a facelift and was made to resemble Mary. And Mary had a similar surgery before she went into hiding."

Selena nodded. It was a fantastic story—but she understood the lengths Don Donovan's wife had been driven to.

"Mary had agreed to stay hidden, but couldn't resist trying to make Donovan insane. I pitied her then. Of all that she'd seen, she should've known he was already insane."

Mary continued, moving away as if she were deep in thought. "I thought I would go mad from living in that house everyday."

"It's killing you not knowing if Andrew if he inherited his cruelty or if he chose that life," Selena said. Or if he was Mary's son, she added silently. She saw a movement and stopped, carefully checking out the situation.

A voice rang out, "Selena, it's us. Mack and me."

Mack, carrying Eric, and Drake waited at the end of the trail. Larry and Martha followed. Mack drew Mary into his arms immediately, keeping distance from Larry. If Selena didn't know better, she'd swear it was a mutual agreement between Martha and Mack. Larry seemed as if he had several bones to pick. It didn't take long for it to spill as they walked back to the Christmas festivities.

"That was a mighty expensive gift you gave my wife," Larry said.

"Someone owed me a special favor and I called it in, requesting the delivery as a priority." Drake added a blanket to Selena's shoulders.

Larry was visibly fighting for words. "Dammit. Did you have to make it purple? Next week, my car goes in the shop."

Drake and Martha high-fived.

Larry tapped Martha on the shoulder. "Can you tell me why we're staying in Selena's home and not our own?"

Martha considered Larry's question a moment and then smiled. "Honey ... Do you remember when your mother retired and decided to travel and for three years we never heard from her? Well, living in Selena's home will give us that opportunity. So, I arranged to swap deeds with Drake."

"I don't get it," Larry said, having turned to watch the deer.

"You will," Martha told him.

Selena heard the sound of footsteps crunching in the snow. She turned and saw Mrs. Irons and Duke. Selena began introducing Mrs. Irons to the others, but Martha stalled her.

"We've met," Martha said with a laugh and hugged Mrs. Irons. "Larry, guess who came to dinner."

"Damn. Sorry, Mom, but damn," Larry said.

Everyone laughed except Larry.

Drake hugged Selena close. As they walked back to cabin, huge snowflakes fell, covering the hard ground. Selena couldn't stop wondering if Mary had answers to—

Drake kissed the top of head and swept her into his arms.

"Don't even think of it," he warned.

"Do you know how much I love you?" she whispered for his ears only.

"I know I love you too much to underestimate you. Tonight I'll show you how much I love you."

And he would.

In the mood for more Crimson Romance? Check out *Necessary Evil* at CrimsonRomance.com.

www.ingramcontent.com/pod-product-compliance
Lightning Source LLC
Chambersburg PA
CBHW010639100726
47900CB00011B/2900

* 9 7 8 1 4 4 0 5 5 1 6 7 3 *